Philip Lovel is a retired Metropolitan police officer. He was born and brought up near Upton-on-Severn, Worcestershire, before moving to Great Malvern. He has since done voluntary work of various types and now lives in Surrey. He is married with two grown-up children, and his interests include history, ornithology, meteorology, and the occasional glass of wine.

To Angela

Philip Lovel

THE TRIBULATIONS OF MISS GLASS

AUSTIN MACAULEY PUBLISHERS™

LONDON * CAMBRIDGE * NEW YORK * SHARJAH

A CIP catalogue record for this title is available from the British Library.

ISBN 9781398434394 (Paperback)
ISBN 9781398434400 (ePub e-book)

www.austinmacauley.com

First Published 2022
Austin Macauley Publishers Ltd®
1 Canada Square
Canary Wharf
London
E14 5AA

Chapter 1

'Leticia, what are you doing to that cat?'

'Nothing, Mama.'

'Don't lie to me, child, you're pulling its tail, stop it.'

Leticia Glass turned her back and stuck out her tongue as the cat ran off down the garden of the large Victorian villa and disappeared into some bushes.

'Really, that child,' Mrs Glass remarked later to the girl's father, 'I don't know what gets into her.'

'Well, if she does it again I will deal with her severely,' he replied.

Mr Glass was seldom at home being frequently away on business and on his return was often obliged to deal with a litany of complaints regarding his nine-year-old daughter.

It was on such an occasion that her mother complained bitterly about Leticia's latest escapade.

Mr Glass sighed.

'All right, what has happened this time?'

'I caught our wretched daughter beating the cat with a stick, the poor animal was yowling at the top of its voice and when I told her to stop, she just continued until I physically removed the stick from her.'

'Go and get her, this has got to end.'

Leticia appeared a few moments later looking sullen and refusing to look her father in the eye.

'Have you got an explanation for your atrocious behaviour towards the cat, Leticia?'

The girl shrugged.

'I asked you to explain, kindly do so immediately.'

The girl still said nothing.

'Do you want me to beat you?' he demanded angrily.

Still no reply.

'Then you leave me with no alternative.'

Glass marched to his study desk and opening the drawer produced a long cane and beat his daughter four times.

'Now go to your room, child, there will no supper for you tonight, next time it will be worse.'

The weather in the summer holidays of 1897 was mixed and the swimming pool at the house, expensively installed some years previously, had seldom been used even during warm weather but that changed one day, when the heat drove Mr Glass to sunbathe, his wife and son having taken the dog cart to Leominster. Leticia meanwhile moped about the garden unable to make up her mind as to what to do. Eventually the heat drove her father to venture into the pool but slowly and reluctantly as he was a non-swimmer. A moment or two later he suddenly cried out in pain, clutched his chest and struggled to get out.

'Help me, Leticia, please, I am unwell.'

About fifty yards away the girl stood motionless as her father continued to cry for help but eventually weakening and unable to keep his feet, slid slowly under the water.

'What's going on, Miss Leticia?' a voice called. 'Did I hear someone call for help?'

It was Harris, the gardener, who was hurrying up a nearby path.

'It's my father, he's in the pool, I think he's ill.'

'Get down to Doctor Brown in the village,' instructed the man.

Leticia hesitated.

'Don't just stand there, girl, run.'

Harris then hurried to the pool jumped in and dragged Glass to the side.

After about twenty minutes, the doctor appeared on his bicycle.

'It's too late, he's gone,' he concluded as he examined Glass's body, which the gardener with some considerable effort had managed to drag out of the pool.

'What happened here, Harris?' he asked.

'Well, sir, I heard, Mr Glass shouting, like, and I came running but it were too late he were dead in the pool face down. If only I had got here sooner.'

'You've nothing with which to reproach yourself. So what was the girl doing?'

'Well, she were just standing there, rooted to the spot, like.'

'Go down the village, Harris, and call the police, they'll have to be notified. I'll take the child into the house; we'll wait for them there.'

'Very good, sir.'

Thirty or so minutes later, the front doorbell of the house rang loudly.

'Inspector Moon, Leominster police, the local constable has just told me there's been some sort of an accident,' announced the portly, uniformed figure to the maid.

'All a bit odd, inspector,' said Doctor Brown in the garden after introducing himself, 'seems that the girl just stood there doing nothing, she's only about nine but could have shouted for help.'

'I'll speak to her in the house,' said Moon,' don't want to talk to her by her father's body. You'd better come with me, doctor, if you wouldn't mind.'

'Tell me what happened, child?' the inspector asked in the hallway.

'He was in the pool and said that he was ill,' replied the girl.

'Oh, did he now, so why didn't you go for Doctor Brown straight away or at least speak to Harris?'

'Don't know,' she replied shrugging.

'Where's your mother?'

'Gone to town in the dog cart.'

'All right,' said Moon at length, 'my constable can stay with the girl until her mother gets back, going to come as a hell of a shock.'

'I'll stay as well, inspector,' said Brown, 'I know the family quite well.'

'Right, sir I'll wait for your report, I'll arrange to move the body.'

'Yes, my guess is that it was a heart attack but we'll have to wait for a post-mortem. I don't think inaction from Leticia contributed to his death though but it's strange she doesn't seem to show any feelings about the business, very curious.'

'Got a mean looking face that one,' remarked Moon, 'don't take to her at all.'

Some weeks later an inquest concluded that Glass had indeed died of a heart attack and Leticia was glad.

Chapter 2

A few years later during summer at Cherrywood, a girls' school set deep in the countryside near Hereford, swifts swooped and screamed above the surface of the lake in the extensive grounds as they hunted for food, the windows in the school buildings being wide open due to the stifling heat. It was even too hot to play on the grass tennis courts which had been browned by the sun, but gardeners still laboured and sweated in two large greenhouses and another scythed the long grass nearby. A few senior girls swam in the pool or sat idly on the edge but the junior school sweltered in the classrooms with a promise of a swim later.

Suddenly, there was a commotion and a shout followed by the sound of a child wailing causing the man with the scythe to pause and look up.

'Come quickly, Miss Grey, there's been a terrible accident,' announced a junior teacher bursting into the headmistress's study.

'What on earth has happened, Miss Hunter?'

'One of the girls, Fiona Clerk, has fallen down the main stairs.'

The two women rushed to the hallway where a teacher was attending to a girl lying crumpled up at the bottom of the stairs whimpering and crying.

'Where does it hurt, child?' the headmistress asked.

'My back, Miss Grey,' she replied in a low voice, the tears tumbling down her cheeks.

'All right, try to get up but very slowly, let the bannister take the weight. If it's too painful stay on the stair, understand?'

'Yes, Miss Grey.'

The girl slowly rose to her feet helped by a teacher.

'How does that feel?'

'I think it's all right.'

'Good, but we'll take you to the san so that matron can check you over.'

The headmistress drew Miss Hunter aside.

'You accompany her please, looks like it's just bruising but on another occasion please don't exaggerate such matters it really doesn't help. You made it sound like a murder had been committed.'

'Sorry, Miss Grey, I'll see if I can find out exactly what happened.'

'Yes, please do and report to me as soon as possible, I will have to notify the child's parents so I need to be in possession of the facts.'

An hour later Miss Hunter knocked on the headmistress's door.

'The girl is all right, just a bit of bruising as you thought. But it's all a bit complicated and it seems that Leticia Glass was responsible.'

'Oh, not that child again, she's nothing but a confounded nuisance,' responded Miss Grey.

'Yes, well it seems that there was some jealousy over another girl between Leticia and Fiona Clerk, the girl who fell, and according to Margaret Cameron and Olive Adams who are friends of Fiona, Leticia pushed the girl down the stairs in a fit of temper. Stephanie Smith, it seems also saw what happened but she's not saying much at present other than it was Leticia.'

Miss Grey sighed.

'Oh dear, any other witnesses?'

'No, just Margaret and Olive and of course Stephanie but there may be others who are reluctant to come forward. Fiona doesn't know who the culprit is, she just felt a hand in the small of her back.'

'Are these girls reliable do you think?'

'Impossible to say, headmistress, you know what schoolgirls are like.'

'And what about Leticia?'

'Well, she denies it, of course but as we are aware she's a well-known liar and not very popular to boot. Says she wasn't anywhere near the stairs.'

'I've telephoned Fiona's parents,' said Miss Grey, and they are motoring up tomorrow afternoon. I'm not looking forward to it as we may lose a pupil as a result. We will probably be losing Leticia too given this incident and her previous behaviour. I plan to expel her unless a satisfactory alternative explanation emerges. I've spoken to her mother who is coming tomorrow morning at 10 a.m. So please arrange for Leticia to be in my study at 10.15 a.m., that will give me a chance to chat to Mrs Glass beforehand.'

'No Mr Glass then?'

'No, that may be part of the trouble, apparently he died a year or two ago, supposed to have drowned in his swimming pool.'

'We require the fullest explanation, Miss Grey,' Mr Clerk was saying a moment or two after their arrival the following morning. 'I'm very unhappy with the whole affair and I'm sure you realise this may lead to our removing Fiona from the school?'

'I understand entirely, Mr Clerk, we think we know who's responsible and the school will be taking the appropriate action in consultation with the school governors.'

'And what is the culprit's name?'

'I'm sorry I'm not at liberty to divulge that until I've spoken to them later this afternoon and a decision on the girl's future has been made.'

'All right, so long as effective action is taken, now kindly conduct us to the san so that we may speak with our daughter.'

The following day, despite denials from the girl, Leticia Glass left the school for good accompanied by her mother.

The expulsion caused some domestic difficulty and the immediate lack of an available replacement school resulted in the girl having to be educated at home with a succession of tutors who regarded Leticia as a bright but unpleasant and difficult child. Eventually a school was found in Hereford and there the girl remained until, following successful completion of her examinations, she left in the summer of 1907 to take up a junior English teaching job at the Abbey School, Malvern.

Chapter 3

At the Abbey, Leticia Glass, despite her relative youth, soon gained the reputation as a martinet and pupils and colleagues alike avoided disagreements with her if they could. Lavinia Brown, the headmistress, occasionally wrung her hands in exasperation and had once considered dismissal but nevertheless many children succeeded under the young teacher's tutelage even if only through fear and as a result, the headmistress and most parents reluctantly tolerated her methods.

Some years later in early autumn, she was unexpectedly called to the headmistress's study.

'I'd like to ask you something, Miss Glass. Tell me, do you know anything about other girls' schools in Malvern and the surrounding area?'

Leticia Glass was puzzled, not entirely sure as to Miss Brown's meaning.

'Er, I think very little, headmistress.'

'My point precisely, we know nothing of their curricula, their teaching methods, what they expect of their pupils and so on, even what sports they play. I therefore plan to do something about it. I propose arranging a gathering of headmistresses and their deputies here at the school to talk over the issues and as a result perhaps we can all benefit from an exchange of ideas and I want you to be involved. You're rather young and have a reputation of being a disciplinarian but you're experienced and good at your job and know what you're talking about. I would normally ask my deputy to assist but as you know she is leaving at the end of term and I don't wish to put too much on the shoulders of her replacement too soon and as one of our senior staff that's where you come in. We'd probably only meet once or twice a year. You would represent the school in the event of me not being available and I would certainly want you present at the first meeting. What do you think?'

'Well, it's a promising idea, Miss Brown, have you put out any feelers yet?'

'Yes, one or two, the Girls' College and Ellerslie seem to be in favour, I don't know about the others yet.'

The meeting was set for later that term and when the day arrived, headmistresses from various schools in and around the Malvern area gathered over tea in the staff room at the Abbey School.

Leticia Glass was chatting with guests when a voice loudly interrupted the conversation.

'Ah, Leticia Glass isn't it? I heard you were here, so many years have passed since Cherrywood, don't you think?'

Glass swung around. 'Do I know you?'

'Yes, don't you remember, Stephanie, Stephanie Smith, I was at the school when you were supposed to have pushed that girl down the stairs. Of course I know you didn't do it but still these things happen at school and children do tell untruths don't they?'

'I do not wish to be reminded of that incident, Stephanie, and especially not now, do I make myself clear?' Glass replied angrily, her face darkening.

Heads began to turn.

'Well, there's no need to be quite so off hand, Leticia, I was just trying to be friendly that's all,' replied the woman turning away shocked.

'Is everything all right, Miss Glass?' asked the headmistress who was hovering anxiously nearby.

'Yes of course, Miss Brown, just a misunderstanding from long ago that's all,' replied the teacher.

Stephanie Smith opened her mouth but thinking better of it said nothing further.

The meeting over, Miss Glass was approached by the headmistress.

'I think the proceedings can be deemed a success,' she said, 'we must therefore do what we can to build on this initial enthusiasm. And by the way, I hope there's no bad feeling between you and Stephanie Smith, she's headmistress over at Bushley school near Queenhill, quite good apparently. So please if you have any disagreements with her kindly keep them separate from school business.'

'Yes of course Miss Brown, I understand.'

Leticia Glass returned to her room and seethed but there was something interesting that Stephanie had said which gave her pause for thought.

'You were supposed to have pushed that girl down the stairs' and 'children tell tales.' And most tellingly of all 'I know you didn't do it.' She was intrigued despite her anger. Stephanie confirmed that lies had been told that day the result being that she, Leticia, had had to live with the consequences ever since. So this might be an opportunity to clear her name as she believed that the incident had affected her career. Yes, she had been desperately unpopular at Cherrywood and, yes, she had said and done things she regretted but she had not pushed that child and Stephanie Smith had confirmed that. Come hell or high water she would have it out with the woman and, if necessary, make her and the others involved apologise even after such a length of time. Such was the nature of Leticia Glass.

Therefore, the following Sunday morning not being required for church duties she determinedly climbed into her car and driving at her accustomed speed tore along the narrow lanes that led from Upton to Bushley School arriving in a shower of dust and gravel as pupils were returning from church service at Queenhill. She leapt out of the car and rang the bell on the heavy front door.

'May I speak to Miss Smith, please?' she enquired of the doorman.

'Have you an appointment, madam?'

'No, I haven't,' she replied rather abruptly her right foot tapping impatiently on the doorstep.

'Well, just a moment, madam, she's just returned from church I'll see if she's available, what name shall I give?'

'Leticia Glass from the Abbey School, Malvern.'

'Wait here a moment, please.'

After a few minutes the man returned, 'Miss Smith will see you now, this way.'

'Hello Leticia, this is unexpected, especially after our contra temps a day or two ago,' remarked Stephanie Smith pleasantly as the visitor was ushered into her study.

'Anyway that aside, I presume this is about the next stage of the schools' co-operation programme? But I'd prefer you to have made an appointment, Leticia, I am rather busy. I'm surprised Miss Brown didn't insist upon it.'

'Miss Brown doesn't know I'm here and it's nothing to do with the schools' programme.'

The headmistress looked startled.

'I don't think I like the sound of this, Leticia, what is the purpose of your visit?'

'Cherrywood.'

'Cherrywood?' the headmistress asked incredulously.

'Yes, Cherrywood, the day that Fiona whatever her name was, was pushed down the stairs.'

'Do you mean to say that you've come all the way over here and interrupted my working day just so that you can talk about an incident that occurred all those years ago at Cherrywood?'

'You wretched, hypocritical woman,' exploded Glass, 'because of you and those other children, I was wrongfully accused of pushing that girl down the stairs with all the consequences that followed and then you turn up years later and make casual remarks in front of people as if you were talking about your summer holidays. And what is more having presumably been instructed to lie which added to the pressure on the headmistress to expel me, when it came to it, you didn't even come forward at the last minute to admit what you had done. You were told to lie, weren't you? WEREN'T YOU?'

The headmistress jumped slightly then sighed.

'Look, Leticia,' said Miss Smith, her tone softening, 'I realise I was a bit tactless the other day, it was entirely the wrong time to mention the matter and I'm sorry. I suppose I somehow thought you might have learnt who the culprits were. And yes, I was pressured into lying, I know it was wrong but I was just a child.'

'So who were the others involved?'

'Nothing can be gained from knowing that, not after all this time.'

'I want to know, Stephanie, and I want to know immediately,' insisted Glass angrily, 'it may not matter to you but those children had me expelled and it's on my record for all to see, even now. If you had spoken up at the time, it might have saved the situation and I would have been a head of school somewhere by now if it hadn't been for that incident.'

'You don't know that, Leticia,' replied Smith 'and besides, I was timid and frightened of getting into trouble.'

'I DO know, so who was it that pushed Fiona and who told the staff that it was me?'

Miss Smith sighed.

'All right if you must know, it was Margaret Cameron who pushed the child and Olive Adams who said that it was you. They were both in it together. I happened to be near the stairs when it happened and they persuaded me to lie, I was a bit frightened of them. You were not very popular and they just wanted to get you into trouble. Poor Fiona ended up being injured because the others knew that you and she didn't get on and that you'd probably get the blame. She was the scapegoat in all this and didn't know that Margaret was responsible.'

'Believe me, I think I was the scapegoat so where are they now, Stephanie, do you know?'

'Oh, for heaven's sake you're surely not thinking about getting some sort of revenge now, Leticia, after all these years. It was a stupid schoolgirl prank that went wrong, surely you must realise that? And no, I don't know where Olive is now but apparently Margaret died of cholera overseas somewhere and I've not the remotest idea where Fiona is either so will you please go as I have work to do. And kindly desist from such unofficial visits in the future otherwise I will have to inform Miss Brown.'

'Inform who you like,' replied Glass and turning on her heel marched out of the study slamming the door behind her nevertheless pondering the answers given by the headmistress. Where was Olive now? Sooner or later, she would find out.

The headmistress thought for a moment then picked up the phone and asked for a number.

'Hello, Olive, this is Stephanie Smith.'

Chapter 4

It was mid-June of 1920 and a match flared in the semi-darkness as Horace Biles lit his pipe and stepped out from the office on his evening round of the Girls' College in Malvern. He was head doorkeeper, had been for two years since old Nicholls retired. It suited him, but the hours were a bit inconvenient at times. It was hardly strenuous work, checking the school buildings and dealing with parents who visited for events such as sports day and the end of term Christmas carol service. Still, only a few years to retirement, then he could do what he really wanted to do: play bowls. The local team had been quite successful that year and he hoped to become more involved. He wanted more of that, not having to worry about whether he could fit his playing around work. Anyway, his wife would be glad to get him out from under her feet.

The school was a private boarding school for girls, originally founded in 1893 elsewhere in the town though now located in what had once been The Imperial Hotel, the railway station being less than a hundred yards away. The line had been a difficult feat of engineering through the local granite and the board of the Great Western Railway teetered on giving up the project on grounds of cost. But the line and the gothic-style station eventually opened in the 1860s. A tunnel connecting the station and the hotel had also been installed in 1862 so as to allow convenient access to the hotel for first class passengers.

The drawback was the constant noise from the railway which kept many awake, especially new arrivals, and eventually the hotel, a large rambling Victorian building, had run out of money and had been bought in 1919 and turned into a successful school. A portrait of the two founding ladies, a bit severe some thought, hung on a panelled wall directly opposite the front door of the school, seemingly casting a quizzical eye upon all those who entered. But now the place was prospering under the tutelage of a new headmistress, Dorothy Sweet. She was young, in fact much younger than the school governors might have wished on her appointment, especially some of the older members. However, it turned out to be an inspired choice, not merely because she was a new broom but also a

18

woman with practical ideas, which gradually overcame early resistance shown by a few, particularly older, members of staff. But they were soon won over, and now there was a long waiting list for prospective pupils.

That evening, thunder rumbled, especially to the north, and the occasional lightning flash lit up the sky. It was sultry and people were still walking around in shirt sleeves even though it was the middle of the evening. Biles shivered despite the warmth, thunder reminded him too much of the guns on the Western Front. It made him feel vulnerable and he dreamt bad dreams; too many men, too many mates, had died. He'd been one of the lucky ones, having been invalided out of the army in 1917, some three years before with a leg injury, leaving him with a slight limp. He had wanted to be a physical training instructor but his wound had put paid to that. He had worked on the railway for a while as a porter at Malvern Link but didn't like the job and had eventually got the post of head doorkeeper at the college.

A local passenger train pulled out of the station with much fuss and blowing of its whistle and rumbled away up the line towards Worcester, the glow from the firebox visible above the cutting, the signal to the north of the station clattering loudly back into position as the train passed. Biles completed his checks of the buildings, the few lights showing coming from the school staffroom and corridors. The junior pupils were completing their prep and would soon be going to bed. Some of the senior girls were still around but, except for the head girl and her deputy, were not allowed out of the school building after 8 p.m. He glanced up at the school clock perched in a cupola on the roof and checked the time against his pocket watch. The clock was, as usual, five minutes fast. It was wound and adjusted once a week but somehow it never kept proper time, but at least electric light had been installed so that it could be seen on the darkest of nights. As he returned to the office by the main door of the school, there was the sound of footsteps on the gravel drive.

'Good evening, Mr Biles,' said a voice.

It was Miss Sweet, the headmistress.

'Oh, good evening, miss, I wasn't expecting to see you.'

'Well, I'm off for a late walk to clear my head before doing some more end-of-term work.'

'I think it's going to rain; you might get very wet and the lightening could be dangerous, especially if you're going up into the hills,' cautioned the man.

19

'Don't worry, Mr Biles, I'm not sure where I'm going yet but I've got my raincoat, umbrella and wellies, I'll be fine,' she called as she disappeared into the gloom and out of the school gate.

The headmistress often walked late to recharge her batteries, and that day had been particularly trying because of continuing disagreements with her deputy, Leticia Glass. In fact, there had been quite a row that afternoon, one of many that had occurred since Miss Sweet's appointment a couple of years previously. This particular argument centred on the freedom of Glass to adjust the curriculum without reference to Miss Sweet. The headmistress insisted that she be informed and that nothing should change without reference to her. It was now getting to the point where consideration might have to be given to dismissing the woman, but Miss Sweet was reluctant to set this in train for fear of losing a good teacher and a capable administrator.

The nub of the problem originally lay with the fact that Miss Glass had applied for the post of headmistress at Malvern College and almost every other school in Malvern but had failed to be appointed and she had never quite accepted the fact. Despite her talents, she considered herself to be a failure and much of the responsibility for that, she, Leticia, thought lay with other people. But Miss Sweet continued on her walk, determined to put the day's events behind her, at least for the time being, despite the thunder and increasing rain.

As the evening wore on and it started to get dark rather earlier than usual under threatening clouds, drops of heavy rain began to fall, and as Biles shut the door of his office, there was a particularly loud clap of thunder and it began to rain in torrents, hammering on the windows, one of which started to leak as it usually did in heavy rain.

'Oh, dear, the headmistress will get wet; I wonder where she is.'

Biles examined his pocket watch anxiously, it was ten past nine.

Meanwhile, the deputy headmistress screeched past the front door in her car to a parking space by the headmistress's study, gravel thrown up from the tyres clattering on the lower windows of the office.

'Dreadful woman, I hope she gets soaked when she gets out,' said Biles to Thomas Welcome, his night relief who had just come on duty. 'I don't know what's happened to Miss Sweet, she went out for a walk and isn't back yet.

'Well, I'm off home,' he continued, 'if I don't get drowned on the way,' and donning his waterproofs, Biles climbed on his bike and disappeared into the rain and the night.

Welcome settled down into his chair as water from the window continued its rhythmic drip into a metal bucket kept for the purpose. At the rate the rain was coming down, he reckoned it would soon have to be emptied.

Thinking on what old man Biles had said, Welcome admitted to himself he didn't like Glass either, for more than once he had suffered the sharp end of her tongue.

'A much nicer class of woman, Miss Sweet,' he said to himself, 'and with a bit of luck, Glass will soon move on.'

At precisely ten o'clock, Miss Stubbs, the duty housemistress, opened the staff room door and started her evening round by climbing the wide Victorian staircase and walking along an oak-panelled corridor on the way to the junior dormitories. On arrival, however, nothing stirred despite the thunder and she retraced her steps, this time to the upper floor where, by now, the senior girls should be going to bed. Occasional lightning flickered and cast odd shapes on the ill-lit walls and ceiling as she went. She would be glad when the storm had passed.

'Good night, Miss Stubbs,' said a voice.

It was Tricia Hardman , the head girl, whom she could barely make out in the gloom. Miss Stubbs jumped slightly, she disliked this part of the school, which she considered dark and cold at the best of times, and there were rumours of a ghost although she tried to persuade herself that it was all nonsense.

'Oh, good night, Tricia.' she responded, 'everything all right?'

'Yes, I think so, Miss Stubbs, I'll see you in the morning. I hope the thunder doesn't keep us all awake, some of the girls are a bit frightened.'

'Well, come down to the staff room if they don't settle and I'll come back up and talk to them.'

'Very well, Miss Stubbs.'

The woman then returned to the ground floor, and in so doing passed the headmistress's study. A light shone under the door as it often did and the housemistress called out that everything was settled. There was no reply. There was also no sign of Miss Glass in her study, but she was probably walking around the school as she often did; some said to try and catch the duty housemistress asleep in the staff room. Traditionally, Miss Sweet would not invite a teacher into her office on these occasions and thus Miss Stubbs returned to the staff room. The clock read 10:21 p.m. and she sighed, she could not go off duty until midnight but still had to be up early the following morning, both to be at assembly and to teach the eccentricities of the French language to a reluctant Form B. She intended to do some marking but decided she was too tired and read a book instead. She then did another tour of the school before midnight, which arrived quicker than she hoped, and locking the staff room door, went to bed. She would rather have gone to her room in one of the buildings in the grounds reserved for teacher accommodation but was required to sleep in the main school in case of emergency. But it saved her a walk, although the thunder was fading now and the rain was less heavy.

Earlier, as Miss Sweet reached Thurrock's quarry, normally one of her favourite walks, it started to rain more heavily and lightning flashed around the hills with constant thunder.

'Perhaps this was not such a good idea after all,' said the headmistress to herself and she pondered whether she should turn back. But rain or no rain, a short walk along the quarry path would be fine and she would then return to the school, and she had her little torch. As she put on her mac, the quarry hut came into view and growing closer, she could hear loud grunting sounds issuing from inside despite the thunder but could not make them out. She intended to walk by but curiosity made her pause, and retracing a couple of steps, she pushed at the door, which after some resistance, came open. She looked inside and shone her light.

Chapter 5

The following morning, the usual frenetic pre-assembly activity had taken over the school. In the staff room, the deputy head, Leticia Glass, glanced at her watch.

'Anyone seen Miss Sweet this morning?' she asked.

Everyone shook their heads.

'Odd,' said the deputy headmistress, 'she's normally here by now.'

Assembly took place at nine sharp and Miss Sweet always attended; she considered assembly one of the few occasions when she could address all the girls.

'Please be so good as to go and check her study and take the spare key with you,' said Miss Glass, addressing a junior teacher, Margery Webb. But the latter soon returned with a puzzled expression on her face.

'There's no sign of her, Miss Glass, her study is locked as it usually is when she's not there. But the light's still on and there's a window open which I closed in case it rains again.'

The deputy head hesitated, it was nearly nine and the pupils were making their noisy way to the school hall.

'Right, I will take assembly,' she said, 'then we must search for her. Anyone not involved immediately in teaching class please return here afterwards, I may need your help if Miss Sweet hasn't appeared.'

Thirty minutes later, there being no sign of the headmistress, Miss Glass called a council of war in the staff room.

'Miss Stubbs, was the head in her study last night when you did your rounds?'

'I presume so but I don't actually know,' she replied, 'I called out to her in the normal way as I passed, and there was no acknowledgment but that's not unusual; the light was on and it was still on during my final round.'

'Well, go and check her lodgings and anywhere else you can think of then come back here and let me know if there's any sign of her, and also speak to Mr

Biles, see if he can help. She presumably went out for her walk as she said she was going to do and she certainly wasn't here when I got back. I'm going to have another look at her study, the rest of you carry on as normal and I'll let you have any news when I get it. Miss Webb, come with me please.'

There was nothing untoward about the study, everything was normal. Miss Sweet was a meticulously tidy woman, a trait that Miss Glass envied. The previously open window had left a pool of water on the floor where the rain had come in.

'Well, it all looks very normal, except for the light being left on, which suggests that she never returned after her walk. I notice that her car's still there and the access door to the outside is locked, which is as it should be. This is all very odd; I wonder what on earth has happened? Perhaps she's been taken ill or something.'

'There's no sign of the head at her lodgings and I've had a look in the spare lab and classroom one, which are both empty, Miss Glass,' said Miss Stubbs, poking her head around the door, 'and I've had a word with Mr Biles but he's just as mystified as we are. He saw her go out for her walk but she didn't return, at least when he was on duty. I suppose it's possible that Mr Welcome saw something.'

Miss Glass looked out of the window, hands on hips, 'I will have to talk to the chairman of the governors,' she said after a long pause, 'eventually we may have to involve the police.'

Margery Webb gave a sharp intake of breath.

'The police?' she exclaimed nervously.

Miss Glass looked slightly annoyed.

'We have to consider every option, you know, Miss Webb, but I hope Miss Sweet will suddenly appear and all will be well.'

The deputy head picked up the phone.

'Switchboard, can you put me through to Colonel Phillips, the chairman of the governors, please?'

After some delay, she spoke to him and explained the situation.

'How quite extraordinary, I'll come over straight away.'

Ten minutes later, the colonel, a red-faced, corpulent man, wearing tweeds and sporting a scarlet pocket handkerchief appeared rather out of breath at the headmistress's study door.

'Any sign of Miss Sweet yet, Miss Glass?'

'No, I'm afraid not, colonel.'

'All right, before involving the police, we need to say that we have looked in in all the likely places,' he said.

'That has been done, colonel,' assured Miss Glass, 'we've looked at her lodgings, and some of the lesser used rooms around the school, but I suppose we'd better check the grounds.'

Thirty or so minutes later, nothing having been found in the latter, Colonel Phillips called the police.

'I've asked them to meet us here in the study,' he said, 'more out of sight here, less fuss, you understand. But I suppose everyone will still see the police cars.'

A few minutes later, there was a knock on the study door.

'I'm Inspector Forbes, Malvern Police,' announced a large and smartly uniformed man standing in the doorway.

'And I'm Colonel Phillips, chairman of the board of governors,' he replied, proffering a hand. 'I'm afraid we have a bit of a problem, inspector, and we'd like your help. Please come in.'

Forbes removed his hat and listened carefully to the train of events.

'There must be a good reason for her disappearance, sir, people usually don't just vanish.'

Phillips bridled slightly.

'I would have thought that was self-evident, inspector, the important question is what happens next?'

'Nothing immediate, sir, we're going to have to wait.'

'Wait, man, wait,' replied the colonel angrily, 'this business is going to be all over the school in a shake of a dog's tail, I want her found as soon as possible.'

'Please calm down, sir, and I will explain.'

The colonel sighed and collapsed heavily into Miss Sweet's chair, which protested under the unaccustomed onslaught.

'All right, carry on inspector.'

'Nine missing persons out of ten turn up within a few hours, sir, so unless there is indication of foul play, we wait.'

'For how long?' the colonel demanded.

'Tomorrow morning, sir, if she has not reappeared by then, we will have to conduct a thorough search and take things on from there. Perhaps you'd be good enough to supply me with her family's details, just in case. Does she live locally, I mean during school holidays?'

'Miss Glass?' asked the colonel, turning enquiringly towards her.

'No,' she replied, 'but I believe she has a house somewhere on the Welsh borders and her parents live in the Hereford area. I'll get the details for you now.'

She got up and rummaged in a nearby cupboard and soon produced an address book from which the inspector took details.

'Thank you, colonel,' said Forbes as he turned for the door, 'either way, please let the station know if there's any news. I will telephone in the morning at about 8:30 a.m. and if she hasn't turned up I will make the necessary arrangements to search the school and anywhere else that may be necessary.'

'I hope it doesn't come to that, inspector,' said Miss Glass, 'I've really no idea where we'll put the girls.'

'Well, I don't think it will be necessary to search the classrooms or dormitories initially, but of particular interest will be her lodgings, the grounds, gymnasium and so on. I'll have a word with your doorman on the way out.'

'Yes, inspector, Biles told me that he saw her setting off for a walk, which is something she quite often did in the evenings but it seems she didn't return.'

'Did you see anything of her late yesterday, Miss Glass?' enquired the colonel.

'Yes, at the end of the afternoon after school finished, we talked over a few things and she went off to her study to work as she usually did. That was the last time I saw her because she told me that she was going out for an evening walk so I didn't see her again. She often got back late from these walks, but she would usually return to her study to work until well after midnight. Generally, I wouldn't disturb her again unless it was important. In any case I went out in my car during the evening so I wasn't here for much of the time.'

'Did she seem normal yesterday?'

'Yes, perfectly, but I should say that we had a slight disagreement yesterday afternoon, but that was settled quite amicably.'

'What was the disagreement about, Miss Glass?' the inspector enquired.

'Oh, over administrative arrangements and other matters, nothing dreadfully serious.'

'Are such disagreements commonplace?' enquired the inspector.

'They happen from time to time but they are mostly amicable.'

There was a barely audible grunt from Colonel Phillips, which attracted a glance from Forbes but he did not pursue the matter.

After taking some notes, the inspector nodded his thanks and left.

'Well, I don't think I can do anything useful by remaining here,' announced the colonel, 'let me know at home immediately if there's any news, Miss Glass. If the girls start asking questions, I suggest we say that Miss Sweet is ill and leave it at that, some of them will have seen the inspector but that can't be helped.'

Members of staff involved returned to the staffroom to be met with a clamour of questions. After explanations, an air of quasi normality slowly descended upon the school but it was another oppressive day with heavy overcast skies and the threat of further thunder. By the end of lessons at four o'clock, there was still no sign of the headmistress.

Miss Glass spoke to the colonel on the telephone.

'Much as I don't like it,' he said, 'we will have to leave it until the morning as the inspector advised, but it's not looking good.'

Leticia Glass was in the headmistress's study and had just put the phone down when there was a knock on the door. It was Tricia Hardman, the head girl.

'Please excuse me for interrupting you, Miss Glass,' she said, 'but there are rumours in the school that Miss Sweet has disappeared and nobody knows where she is, some even say that she has been murdered.'

'Well, you can scotch that nonsense straight away, Tricia,' said Miss Glass, 'we believe Miss Sweet to be ill and kindly be good enough to inform the girls of that should they enquire.'

'But the policeman, Miss Glass, what was he doing here?'

Miss Glass sighed.

'That is a matter for the school at the moment, I'm sorry but I'm not in a position to offer any further explanation at the moment. Please inform the pupils, if asked, that the policeman was here on a routine visit. If I have further news I will let you know.'

The girl reluctantly left but with furrowed brow.

That night, Miss Glass tossed and turned and worried, sleeping only fitfully though the heat and intermittent thunder before dawn arrived all too soon. After breakfast, however, there being no sign of Miss Sweet, she spoke again to Colonel Phillips.

'I'm afraid we are going to have to bow to the inevitable and involve the police,' announced the colonel. 'I'll ring Inspector Forbes. Meanwhile, the business of the school will have to continue in as normal a fashion as possible, and please don't make any announcements without consulting me first; I will have to speak to my fellow governors. And if possible, please put aside any teaching commitments you may have today.'

Just after assembly, a police car and van drew up in front of the school entrance and Inspector Forbes led the way with a uniformed sergeant.

'Good morning, sir,' said Biles, 'I've been asked to direct you to the headmistress's study, Colonel Phillips is waiting for you.'

'OK, sarge, go and tell the lads in the van to stay in there for ten minutes until we've sorted out a plan of action, and then you come to the study; I hope it won't take long.'

'Right then, let's get cracking,' said the inspector after the sergeant had reappeared. 'Take four PCs and search the grounds, particularly that copse by the railway line and anywhere else where there's any natural cover. I will take a constable and concentrate on the buildings; we can meet back here in an hour or so unless we find something.

'Colonel, I've been in touch with Miss Sweet's family,' continued the inspector, 'they haven't seen her for several weeks and are obviously concerned. If she does turn up, naturally they'll let us know. Meanwhile, apart from the gymnasium and the swimming pool, is there anywhere in the main school building that is not often visited?'

The colonel scratched his head and puffed out his cheeks.

'Well, let me think, there's the boiler room, not much visited, especially at this time of the year, there's the clock tower and lofts, oh, and the passageway to the station, but it's only used at half term or at the end of term to get the girls and their luggage safely to the station. We also looked at the spare lab and classroom one, which is currently out of use and hidey holes including the covered way to the station yesterday but, of course, found nothing. I should point out that there is also a well in the kitchen garden but it's covered in, and by the look of it hasn't been disturbed in years.'

'Right, we'll double check these places just in case,' said the inspector. 'Miss Glass, perhaps you could act as my guide?'

'Yes, of course, we'll go to the boiler room first.'

28

But as the morning went on, it was clear that no progress was being made and the inspector became increasingly gloomy.

'I will have to consult my senior officer,' he said back in Miss Sweet's room, 'but I don't think any further searching here is going to yield results unless we get information to indicate otherwise. By the way, I've had a look at her car, nothing much in there either. The inside is not wet so it probably has not been driven since the rain started yesterday.'

'How did you get in? There's no sign of the key, she must have it with her.' Miss Glass enquired somewhat surprised.

'We have our methods, madam,' he said without a trace of a smile, jangling a mixed bunch of car keys in front of her.

'Anyway, the next stage will be to formally interview staff here and her family and friends to try and find some common ground. Perhaps I could start with you, colonel, can you tell me what she was like, both personally and professionally?'

'Professionally, top ho, but I don't know much about her personal life,' said Phillips, 'she keeps herself very much to herself. Unmarried, of course.'

'Any man friends, sir?' The inspector enquired.

'None that I know of. Miss Glass, are you aware of anyone?'

The deputy headmistress shook her head.

'Anyone on the staff she was particularly friendly with?'

'Well, said Miss Glass, 'I suppose I was her closest confidante at the school, but as deputy head that was purely relating to school matters. She never discussed her private life at all and I never asked about it. I don't think I would describe myself as a close friend. We never met socially except at the end-of-term drinks party with the staff; even then it was mostly just small talk.'

'How long has she been here?'

'Oh, about 18 months in all,' replied the colonel, 'never had any complaints, but I think some of the older staff grumbled amongst themselves for a while. New broom and all that, but they soon settled down when they realised how efficient she was.'

Leticia Glass opened her mouth as if to speak but said nothing.

'No enemies then, would you say?' The inspector went on.

'No, not at all, at least as far as this place is concerned, and I can't imagine anywhere else either come to that.'

'You mentioned that Miss Sweet liked to go for walks, any idea where?'

'As a matter of fact, she liked to walk up at Thurrock's quarry, or sometimes around the town, particularly Priory Gardens, but heaven knows where she went the day before yesterday,' said Miss Glass.

'All right, we must start to interview your staff as soon as they are available and I'll need to contact any of her friends locally that you know of, so I'll need your help with addresses of these and also details of any staff that have left since Miss Sweet arrived. Also, I'll need to borrow a couple of rooms for conducting interviews if that's possible rather than doing it all down the station and we'll need to take statements. It may worry the girls, but I'm sure they are aware that something is going on anyway.

'Incidentally, was Miss Sweet likely to have been carrying a handbag?' queried the inspector.

'Oh, yes,' replied the deputy head, 'she never went anywhere without one.'

'Can you describe it?'

'Well, she had at least two handbags, one of which had a long strap and I think that's probably the one she took with her as it isn't in her study or lodgings. I seem to remember it's got two silver mounts.'

'All right, I'll check it out with the doorkeeper, he may remember something.'

Two days later, the interviewing, which certainly caused some further consternation amongst the pupils, was complete, but of Miss Sweet there was still no sign.

'We have had a look at Thurrock's quarry and Priory Gardens, including the lake,' reported Inspector Forbes to Miss Glass and Colonel Phillips, 'nothing found in either location, but I'm hopeful that publicity in the Malvern Gazette will trigger people's memories, somebody may have seen her. I've had a word with Biles, but apparently she didn't mention where she was going and the lad Welcome didn't see her return, so it's difficult to know where to search next. Mr Biles does not remember a handbag either, but as it was threatening rain she could have been carrying it under her coat. Anyway, if you think of anywhere else, particularly locally, that Miss Sweet might have visited in the past and where she might have gone for a walk, please let me know.'

Chapter 6

Billy Clover was nineteen and worked as a groundsman at the girls' school. He was a hard worker when sober, but he liked a drink, in fact he could be downright unpleasant if the mood and the beer took him. He had nearly been barred from his local pub, The Star, and on that Wednesday evening, some days after Miss Sweets disappearance, he was drinking on borrowed time.

'Remember, said the landlord, 'any trouble tonight and that's it, out you go and you won't be allowed back.'

Clover, who was a big man and towered over him glared but said nothing, and swallowed half of his second pint of bitter.

'I knew her,' he said smirking. 'I knew her, that fancy cow up at the school, the one that's gone missing.'

'There's no need to be like that,' said a man standing at the saloon bar next to him, 'she may be in trouble.'

'So, what if she is?' Clover said, swinging around, his face red and angry.

'All right, all right, I was only saying,' said the man, raising his hands defensively and retreating to another part of the bar.

'Well, I knows a thing or two about her, like I know where she is, she's bloody dead, I know it and it serves her right,' said Clover, tapping the side of his nose knowingly, 'but I'm not telling nobody bloody nothing,' the last word spat with such viciousness that it produced a dribble of spittle from the sides of his mouth.

'Who are you looking at?' He screamed at the landlord, knocking over his glass, with the contents spewing across the bar and on to the floor.

'Right, that's it,' the latter responded, 'you're finished, get out of my pub.'

'Oh, yeah, and what are you going to do, bloody make me?'

'Go now or I'll call the police.'

'I'm not going anywhere,' said Clover, picking up his glass and throwing it at the landlord. The latter ducked, and missing its target, the glass shattered a mirror behind the bar, cascading fragments over a wide area.

'Daisy, call the police,' he said to his barmaid, rushing around the bar and grabbing Clover around the neck.

'Let go, you bastard, I'll bloody kill you,' bellowed the man as he tried to wrestle the landlord to the floor. A few minutes later, police arrived, and Clover, struggling violently, was dragged to a police van, but not before the landlord had punched him hard in the stomach.

'Here, have this one on me,' he said with satisfaction, 'and don't set foot in my pub again.'

Later after closing time, the landlord went to the police station, spoke to the sergeant on duty and related what Clover had said.

'Yes, thank you, Mike, I'll pass it on to Inspector Forbes. We're getting nowhere fast with this Sweet business at the moment and I'm sure he'll want a word with young Clover. He's still sobering up down the cells. Oh, by the way, do you want us to do him for the damage before he goes to court?'

'No, as long as he stays away from my pub. Anyway, he's never got any money except when he wants to buy booze.'

The following morning, Clover was rearrested by a constable outside the court and taken back to the police cells.

''Ere, what's this all about?' protested Clover, 'I'm not drunk no more and I've got a week to pay my fine.'

'It's not about the fine, it's a lot more serious than that.'

Back at the station, Inspector Forbes was waiting for him. 'Stick him down the pokey for a while, I'll talk to him in a few minutes.'

'You can't do this, I ain't done nothing, I've told you I'm sober now,' shouted Clover.

'Go down the cells and keep your mouth shut,' demanded Forbes.

The cell door banged shut just as Chief Inspector Clark appeared.

'I think that DI Pierce better speak to him if there's a chance that Clover has done over that headmistress. This may be moving from a missing person job to possible heaven-knows-what and I've had the chief constable on the phone demanding to know what progress we're making.'

Forbes looked disappointed.

'I was going to have an initial chat with him, sir, then, if necessary, hand over to Jack Pierce after that.'

'No, I think DI Pierce better be involved right at the start, you can sit in on the interview, of course. I hope he can control that Scottish temper of his though.'

Detective Inspector Pierce and Inspector Forbes sat down in the interview room with a nervous looking Clover sitting opposite them.

'Why have I been nicked, why am I here, Mr Pierce?' he asked wearily.

'Right, laddie, you're cautioned and this is the situation,' said the DI. 'A woman, the headmistress, in fact, has disappeared from the girls' school where you work and we think you know where she might be.'

Clover shook his head, 'I know she's been gone these last few days, but I don't know anything about what's happened to her,' he said, shrugging his shoulders.

'Well, now, laddie, we think different, don't we?' pressed the detective inspector, glancing at his colleague.

'Your trouble is that you can't keep your mouth shut, never have, particularly when you've had a few pints. You know where she is, don't you? You were telling everyone in the pub that you did.'

'That was just the drink talking, just the drink,' muttered Clover.

'You're in the mire, laddie, I don't mind telling you, so we'd better start at the beginning again,' continued the DI. 'How about you tell me what you think of Miss Sweet.'

'She were all right, I mean quite nice, really.'

'Were or is?'

'What do you mean were or is?'

Pierce ignoring the reply moved on.

'Oh, she was quite nice, was she, and why do you think that?'

'Well, when I first started work at the school, she welcomed me, like.'

'How was that then?'

'Well, when I were working on the playing fields soon after I started, like, she came up to me and said hello and wished me good luck.'

'Had you ever seen her before?'

'No, it weren't her that interviewed me, like, it were the head groundsman.'

'When did you next see her?'

'Don't know, at various times around the school grounds, I suppose. Look, I don't know nothing, I keep telling you. When do I get a cup of tea and when do I go home?'

Pierce, again ignoring the questions, continued.

'If you think she's all right, why were you mouthing off about her in the pub?'

'I told you, it were the drink talking. I go all stupid when I've had a drink,' said the man.

'Come on, there's more to it than that, stop wasting our time.'

But then a smile suddenly lit up Pierce's face.

'You took a fancy to her, didn't you? She didn't want to know a little toerag like you and you decided to get your own back, that's it, isn't it?'

Clover stared at the table, then suddenly springing up, he lunged at Pierce across the table, trying to grab him by the throat. Forbes pushed the table back hard against Clover, who then fell to the floor his head banging into the wall behind him.

'Get up, laddie, get up,' shouted Pierce, 'try that again and I'll bloody crucify you.'

Clover hauled himself to his feet, holding his head and flopped back dejectedly in the chair. Forbes called for handcuffs and Clover's hands were secured behind his back.

'Well, laddie, you can sweat for a while and count yourself lucky you're not on the sheet for assault. But if you don't cooperate, I may change my mind.'

The youth was then dragged with some difficulty down the passageway to his cell where his handcuffs were removed and the door slammed shut.

'Come on, Bob, I've had enough of this little bastard for the moment, what he needs is a Glasgow handshake to teach him a few manners, let's have a cuppa.'

'So, what do you think, Jack?' asked Forbes when they got back to Pierce's office.

'I dunno, definitely upset him over him fancying her but it's not an offence to take a liking to someone above your station in life, is it? Anyway, we'll let him sweat it out for a bit. Er, mind if I involve Sid next time?'

Sid Bishop was a long-serving detective sergeant at Malvern with a reputation for brusqueness, a lack of humour and not a little violence when the mood took him.

'Fair enough, as long as he doesn't hit him too hard,' rejoined Forbes. 'I'd better get back to what I'm supposed to be doing anyway. Drawn a blank so far with interviewing witnesses, the woman's just disappeared into thin air.'

'Well, Clover's all we've got at the moment,' said the DI, 'when I've had another chat if needs be, I'll get old Sid to start leaning on him a bit and we'll see where we get to.'

Thirty minutes later, the detective inspector returned to the cell accompanied by a detective constable.

'Right, Billy,' said Pierce, 'I don't take offence lightly even though you tried to assault me. So, let's pretend that it didn't happen and start again, eh?'

'No need,' replied Clover glaring, 'I don't know nothing about her, I haven't touched her.'

'Ah, but we think you have,' repeated Pierce, 'you took a fancy to her and she rejected you. Isn't that right?'

'I told you, no,' a note of desperation creeping into his voice.

'All right, when did you last see her?'

'I don't know, I've already said, around the school grounds some time, I suppose.'

'Look,' said Pierce, 'I'm quite a friendly sort really, but we're going around in circles and I'm going to have to get Sergeant Bishop in here and he's altogether a lot nastier than me.'

'Do what you like, I want a solicitor,' growled Clover.

Pierce left and talked briefly to Bishop, who had been poring over some paperwork in the CID office and was immersed in his usual cloud of cigarette smoke, and who then heaved himself out of the chair and walked down the stairs to the cell, a distended belly bouncing rhythmically as he went. He was out of breath by the time he reached the cell, and glancing through the door wicket, entered after it was unlocked by the uniform sergeant.

'My name's Detective Sergeant Bishop, and I've come for a little chat,' he said, slamming the cell door and lowering his huge frame on to the bench seat. 'I don't like talking to people in a cell, it hurts my backside and makes me bad tempered, but you tried to assault my guvnor just now, so this is where we're going to have to stay. But I'm a friendly sort, really, and we'll keep the cuffs off at the moment to prove it. Now I'm going to ask some questions and I want proper answers. Get it?'

'Get what? I ain't done nothing,' insisted Clover.

'Oh dear, oh dear, dear, some people never learn,' said Bishop, standing up and leaning towards the man. Suddenly, Clover doubled up with pain, gasping for breath and shouting as the detective's right fist slammed into his stomach.

'Now that's just for starters, son,' Bishop hissed in Clover's ear, 'now all you've got to do is tell us what a liar and a silly boy you've been and we can be friends, understand?'

Clover rocked backwards and forwards, clutching his stomach and moaning, with tears starting to pour down his face.

'I told you I don't know nothing about the woman,' he gasped, his voice breaking, 'I don't know, I don't know where she is, I never touched her; please don't hit me again.'

Bishop stared at Clover for a second or two then left the cell to consult with Pierce.

'He hasn't coughed, sir, I could whack him again but it may not do any good.'

'Yes, well, I hope nothing will show, Sid.'

'Oh no, sir, nothing will show, nothing will show,' smirked the detective sergeant.

'Problem is,' said DI Pierce, 'we haven't got a shred of evidence against him if he doesn't cough, and if we can't come up with something by morning, we're going to have to kick him out. He hasn't even got many previous, apart from drunk and a couple of malicious damages.'

'Yes, well,' re-joined Bishop, 'it looks like we may have lost this one, sir, certainly as far as he's concerned; I don't think he knows anything about the woman.'

'Possibly, but if we have to release him, sarge,' continued the DI, 'we'll put a tail on him for a while, if he is involved, he might lead us to the woman whether she be dead or alive.'

The following morning after further fruitless questioning, Clover was released without a charge, and although he was followed for several days, nothing came of it, and there being no other lines of enquiry the case eventually lapsed.

Chapter 7

It was mid-June 1937 and one day, the editor of the Malvern Gazette called Diana Davies, a relatively junior stringer, to his office.

'Sit down, Miss Davies, I've got a little job for you.'

'Oh, yes, Mr Robinson.'

'What do you know about Malvern Girls' College?'

'Oh, prestigious and expensive, I think, lost a headmistress as I recall, disappeared a good many years ago now and was never found, was she?'

'No, that's right, Dorothy Sweet, had only been at the school a couple of years, well thought of, just vanished into thin air, no known reason that anyone could come up with. The local police couldn't solve the case and eventually gave up. It's coming up to the seventeenth anniversary of her disappearance and it's about time the paper ran a feature on it. If we leave it for another three years until the twentieth, there may not be too many people left that can remember the incident. You can cast a fresh eye on the newspaper reports of the time, particularly as you weren't here then, see if you can come up with something new. I've also got a contact that you can follow up; Inspector Forbes, the officer in the case. He's retired now, of course, and he's getting on a bit, but he's always maintained an interest, so go and have a chat, here's his address. But before you go, have a look at the county papers of the day, not just ours, to get background. They're in our storeroom. You could also try Jack Bowers who did the original story for us, I can give you his address too but his memory is not so good these days.'

'What about our editor at the time?' queried Davies.

'No luck there, I'm afraid, he's dead and gone some years back.'

The next day, having spent the previous evening looking through the archives, Davies decided that her first call would be on old Mr Bowers. She banged on the yellow door of a cottage perched high above the Wyche Cutting, having puffed up the short but extremely steep path dragging her bike.

'Mr Bowers? I'm Diana Davies from the Gazette, I hope it's convenient to call.'

'Oh, hello, please come in, that's fine I knew you were coming; your boss phoned. It's so nice to have a bit of company.'

'How lovely,' she said, as she was ushered into the sitting room. The cottage and small rose garden looked across Malvern in the foreground and beyond that to rolling fields, which eventually gave way to the valley which lay out of sight below.

'Yes, everybody says that, lived here most of my life and I hope to die here as my late wife did, but it's not so easy getting up the stairs these days or that slope outside, the old rheumatism and all that, please sit down.

'Look, I understand that you're looking into that distressing business with the headmistress. Don't know whether I can help much, my memory is not what it was. Cup of tea?'

'Oh, that would be nice, thank you.'

He returned a few moments later and thrust a cup and saucer into her hand.

'Sorry, I'm not very formal, my late wife would not have been at all impressed with my efforts. Sugar?'

'No, no thanks.'

'Right, where do we start?' the old man asked.

'Perhaps,' Davies ventured, 'we could talk about some of the more important people involved.'

Bowers looked faintly embarrassed.

'I'll try but I'm afraid I don't remember much about them, it was such a long time ago.'

The journalist tried another angle.

'Did you know Miss Sweet before her disappearance?'

'Well, yes, slightly, I visited her at the school for the paper just after she had been appointed, such a nice woman, so cooperative. But I think that was the only time we met, I almost shed a tear when she disappeared.

'As for other people, nothing much sticks. But I did meet a lot of others in the course of the investigation, trouble is I don't remember their names now, except a Miss Glass. I think her name was, yes, Miss Glass, that's right, she was the deputy head at the time. One thing struck me when I talked to her, she didn't seem particularly happy with her lot in life, no idea why, you get a nose for that kind of thing in the newspaper business as I expect you're finding out. She was a little bit brusque, rather a plain Jane too, reluctant to say anything she didn't have to, but maybe that was because she was upset at Miss Sweet's disappearance, although I got the impression that she and Sweet didn't always see eye to eye but nothing specific that I can put my finger on. I imagine, though, she would have mentioned anything important to the police.'

'Yes, I expect so,' acknowledged Davies, 'is there anyone else who springs to mind from those days?'

'No, not that I can recall apart from that old colonel somebody-or-other, chairman of the governors, typical ex-army chap, bit of a blusterer more concerned with the reputation of the school than anything else, not much help really. These schools will insist on using these retired old beggars who haven't a clue how to run an educational establishment. Think they're still in the army and order people about as if they're on the parade ground, that's the trouble.'

'How did he get on with Miss Sweet, do you know?'

'No, I don't know, I'm afraid, but I imagine that she wouldn't have been appointed if the colonel had objected.'

The two chatted some more, then after a while Bowers got up, extending a hand.

'Well, I hate to push you out, young lady, especially as you're from the old firm but I don't think I can be of much more help. Anyway, I suggest you have another talk with Miss Glass if she's still about, dig around a bit, you know what I mean. If you have any luck, I'd love to be kept up to date, and if I think of anything else I'll ring the office.'

'All right, thanks for the tea,' Davies called out as the cottage door closed behind her.

Back at the office, the journalist reported progress to her editor.

'I'm not surprised you didn't get much from Bowers, nice old boy but he's not the man he was,' said Robinson.

'Well, except for a couple of things,' said the girl, 'he thought that Miss Glass had been a bit reluctant to part with information when he interviewed her but couldn't put a finger on it. He also got the impression that Glass and Sweet didn't get on all that well either but nothing specific.'

'Oh, really, I wonder what she was not telling us? I think you must have a word with old Forbes next and also see whether you can trace Glass. I imagine she's still around and young enough to still be working. She might still be in

Malvern, if you can find her, perhaps she might open up a bit, especially given the passage of time.'

Davies examined the phone book and came up with an "S. Glass" but she decided to wait until she had spoken to the retired inspector.

The afternoon of the following day, Forbes and the journalist sat in his garden in West Malvern drinking tea and discussing her visit to Jack Bowers.

'You know I don't especially remember Miss Glass clamming up,' he was saying, 'but it was a long time ago and I spoke to so many people. On the other hand I don't remember her coming up with much useful information either, just going through the motions, I think; didn't take to her much, maybe she was just upset.'

'Yes, that's what Mr Bowers suggested.'

'But I was also wondering whether you spoke to any previous members of staff ?' Davies continued.

'Yes, we interviewed all the teachers we could find who had previously worked at the school but nothing came of it, seems that Miss Sweet was popular with those who knew her although she'd only been at the school about eighteen months before she disappeared, so there were only a few .'

'What about any friends?'

'Didn't seem to have many, we spoke to one or two but they couldn't help.'

'What about this man, Clover? He seems to have been a suspect.'

'Oh, that was just a red herring,' replied Forbes, 'he was just the local drunk, I don't think he had anything to do with it; didn't have the brains. The CID jumped on him because they didn't have anyone else. I mean, they put a watch on him in the hope that he might lead them to Miss Sweet but nothing happened and that was the end of it. No, I think the answer lies elsewhere.'

'What about that old quarry? According to our old newspapers, police searched it but didn't come up with anything.'

'Well, it was me who led the search and I often wonder whether we might have missed something there but nothing suspicious was found and that was that.'

'And the lake in Priory Gardens?'

'We dragged it as a last resort but nothing of course.'

'What about any retired policemen who were involved. Do you keep in touch?'

'No, DI Pierce and DS Bishop lived locally after they retired but they're both gone now. It was the beer that got old Sid Bishop, liked his pints too much plus his fags. Didn't last more than a couple of months in retirement; the job was his whole life. Pierce dropped dead at Bishop's funeral, queer that.'

'So, where to next, I wonder?' queried the journalist.

'That's a matter between you and your editor, but if it were me I'd start again and re-interview Miss Sweet's friends, colleagues and contacts in Malvern, you never know, we might have forgotten something and I don't think the police are likely to re-open the case without some new evidence. But let me know how you get on if you have the time, I'd love to get to the bottom of this before I peg out.'

'Yes, of course, I'll see what I can find out. Oh and thanks,' Davies called out as the door closed behind her and she climbed back on her bike.

The following morning, she rang Malvern Girls' College and spoke to the deputy head.

'My name's Diana Davies from the Malvern Gazette,' she announced, 'and I'm doing a piece on Miss Sweet, your former headmistress. As you may recall, it's about seventeen years since her disappearance and I was wondering whether anyone at the school might know where your predecessor, Miss Leticia Glass, might be now? Is she living in Malvern perhaps? There is a number for someone called Glass in the telephone book but I'd rather speak to somebody at the school first. Also, might you have any contacts among her former colleagues to whom I could speak? Perhaps one or two of them might still be at the school?'

There was a long pause.

'I'm afraid, Miss Davies,' she said, 'I'm not in the habit of providing such information over the phone even if it were immediately available and I'm not sure that it is. I will have to speak to the headmistress and see what she thinks. Ring me back this afternoon and I may have an answer for you.'

An hour later, the phone rang in the editor's office and there was a short conversation.

'Miss Davies,' he called, 'that was the Girls' College, they were checking on your bona fides, no need to ring back, the headmistress is prepared to see you at two o'clock so don't be late.'

Setting off in steady rain and freewheeling most of the way down Avenue Road, she arrived at the school gates a few minutes later and made her way to the imposing Victorian front door which boasted a substantial canopy. She rang the bell which sounded loudly and was soon invited in by the head doorkeeper.

'These places are useful in the rain, miss,' he said, 'would you be Diana Davies by any chance?

'Yes, I have an appointment with Miss Charlton, the headmistress.'

'Oh, yes, she's expecting you, you can leave your bike here if you like, it'll be perfectly safe out of the rain. Straight along the corridor and it's the last door on the left beyond the staircase. Davies nodded and made her way along the passageway with an array of classroom doors on either side from which emerged a mixture of teachers' and pupils' voices, increasing in volume then fading again as she passed by. Large portraits of former headmistresses stared down from panelled Victorian walls, the corridor so gloomy that some were barely discernible. The final portrait next to the headmistress's study door was of Dorothy Sweet, smiling and so much younger than her predecessors, almost inviting the observer to pause and talk with her for a while.

'How sad, how very sad,' the journalist muttered to herself shaking her head.

Davies knocked and was conducted into the headmistress's study by her secretary. A tall, angular figure greeted her and they shook hands.

'Please sit down, Miss Davies, I'm Margaret Charlton. Now, I understand from my deputy and your editor that you're writing a story about that unfortunate business with one of my predecessors?'

'Yes, that's right,' Davies replied, 'as I explained on the phone, I'm trying to contact people who might have been around at the time to see if they can add anything to what we already know.'

'Well, if you're expecting me to provide details of former employees of the school,' mild indignation creeping into Miss Charlton's voice, 'I'm afraid such information is confidential, I couldn't possibly provide it, even if we possess it and we may not. However, I suppose it will do no harm to say that Miss Sweet's deputy, Miss Glass, is still living in partial retirement in Malvern and visits us from time to time, but I can't disclose her address. You will have to do some detective work, but of course as a journalist you'll be used to that. As for Miss Sweet's family, they haven't kept in touch but I believe they live or lived in the Hereford area. Good luck with your investigations, but I'm sure that the police have done all this before and they still haven't discovered the culprit if there was one.'

'Yes, I understand that but did you work with Miss Glass?' enquired the journalist.

'No, she took leave after Miss Sweet's disappearance and the latter's replacement – not me – had been appointed, then obtained another teaching job in Malvern.'

'Thank you, Miss Charlton, but before I go, did you, by any chance, know Miss Sweet?'

'As a matter of fact I did, not very well but I was a junior colleague of hers at another school before her appointment as headmistress here. We weren't close as she was much more senior to me but she was a nice woman, very competent and imaginative too. Her disappearance came as a terrible shock.'

'Did she have any enemies that you know of?'

'I think that's probably beyond your brief, Miss Davies, but I can't imagine that she ever did. She went out of her way to get on with people but she stood her ground when required.'

Realising that nothing further could be gained from the conversation, the journalist thanked the woman and rose to leave.

'Please no overly imaginative journalism, Miss Davies,' called the headmistress as the journalist reached the door, 'it would not be worthy of Miss Sweet's memory.'

The girl nodded and left.

Nothing much to go on, she reflected, as she retraced her steps to the front door, but never mind, at least the woman had given her an interview.

She was about to collect her bike when she had a thought.

'Mr, er, I'm sorry I didn't get your name, ' she said to the doorman, 'I'm a journalist and I've been to see the headmistress about the disappearance of Miss Sweet all those years ago. Did you work here then, and if so, were you on duty that night?'

'Thomas Welcome, miss. Yes, I did and I was here but I didn't see her, she went out before I arrived for work. It was old Mr Biles who saw her, he was head doorkeeper, he's gone now, God rest his soul, but he told everything he knew to the police at the time, as I did. He was very upset, never quite got over it, somehow thought he was to blame. Now, if you'll excuse me, I must attend to my duties, good afternoon.'

Davies cycled back to the office through the drizzle, rechecked the "Gs" and decided to phone the number in the book but there was no reply. If there was no link and Leticia Glass was still in Malvern, she was either ex-directory or simply had no phone. The Hereford listings, however, yielded three possibilities for the Sweet family, each of which would have to be rung to try and establish a link.

That afternoon, an examination of the voters' registers at the library gave the address of a Mr Samuel Glass as in the telephone book, but of Leticia Glass, there was no sign.

'Miss Davies, are you making progress?' boomed Mr Robinson after she had returned from Malvern library.

'Some but not enough, I'm trying to trace people who were around at the time.'

'What about the Glass woman?' he asked.

'Well, I can't find her address,' she replied, 'annoying as the school said she was probably still living in Malvern, but, of course, they wouldn't say where. There's a Samuel Glass, might be related, tried to phone him, couldn't get through. Strangely enough, I couldn't find her in the voters' register, but I suppose she could be listed somewhere else.'

'Well, try Samuel Glass again,' said the editor, pushing the directory across the desk, 'can't do any harm.'

Davies picked up the phone.

'Malvern 55,' said a male voice.

'Please may I speak to Miss Leticia Glass if she's available.'

There was a pause then the phone went dead.

'Well, I'm not sure what that tells us,' remarked the journalist 'but I'll pop up to the address anyway and see if I can get somewhere.'

The house in Graham Road was a fine one, another example of the medium-sized Victorian houses that so abounded in the town. But it had seen better days and its garden was so overgrown with shrubs that some of the ground floor windows suffered from a lack of light. Alarming cracks were also appearing in some of the frames and on the glass with tendrils of ivy trying to force their way in.

Davies rang the bell and the door was opened by a maid. A dog barked and growled murderously in the background.

'I wonder whether I could speak to Mr Glass please?' she enquired of the girl.

'Who is it?' A male voice questioned from inside, the same as on the telephone.

'I'm sorry to trouble you, but my name's Diana Davies from the Malvern Gazette and I'm—'

'Go away,' interrupted a large middle-aged man who appeared at the door elbowing the maid aside, 'I don't trust journalists.'

'I just want to know whether Miss Leticia Glass lives here?' Davies asked loudly above the din.

'Not anymore,' he replied, 'now, for the final time, go away or I'll set the dog on you.'

The journalist left but at least she had established a family connection. The problem was: where was Miss Glass now?

She climbed back on her bike and was about to ride away when she spotted the maid who had answered the door coming down the drive.

'Excuse me,' said Davies.

The maid ignored her and hurried into the road.

'Excuse me,' repeated the journalist, 'I just want a word.'

The girl hesitated and turned around.

'What do you want, miss?'

'I would just like to know where Miss Glass lives, that's all.'

'I shouldn't really tell you,' replied the girl, 'but seeing as I am leaving old misery gut's employment to get married, like, I suppose it don't matter anymore. She lives in Como Road around the corner, number 45, Rose Villa it's called, another big house it is.'

'What's she like?'

'Oh, she's all right, better than that brother of hers but she does have a temper, tore me off a strip more than once I can tell you; I thinks she's a bit funny, like. They don't get on, that's why they live apart. She moved away from the town for a bit but now she's back.'

'Has she got a telephone? I can't find a number.'

'No, but she's going to have one, old man Glass says. Now I must go, I've got to get my mother's tea.'

Davies thanked her and the girl scurried away.

The journalist pondered what to do next. If she tried to visit straight away, she risked being refused an interview. On the other hand, what practical alternative was there, short of a letter? Well, no, she would go around now and take her chances.

It was starting to rain as Davies cycled into Como Road, and finding number 45, leant her bike against a hedge and banged on the door. An elderly butler answered.

'Yes, miss, can I help you?'

'My name's Diana Davies, I wonder whether I could speak to Miss Glass if she's available?'

She had deliberately refrained from mentioning her profession and she thus hoped that the man wouldn't enquire too closely as to her reasons for visiting.

'Just a moment, miss, I will enquire.'

The man soon returned and Davies was conducted into the drawing room where she was greeted by a middle aged, well-built woman with rather piercing blue eyes, her hair in a bun and with slightly protruding teeth. Traces of long hair bristled on her upper lip.

Leticia Glass looked suspicious.

'Well, who are you and what do you want?' she demanded to know.

'My name is Diana Davies and I'm from the Malvern Gazette.'

'Evans, show Miss Davies out, she's leaving,' interrupted Glass loudly, 'why did you let her in?'

'Yes, madam, sorry, madam,' replied the man, slightly flustered.

'This way, Miss Davies,' said the butler, reaching towards her as if to frogmarch her to the door.

'Just a moment, Evans, on second thoughts, let her stay,' said Miss Glass, her tone softening. 'You may sit down, Miss Davies, I don't know why I'm allowing you to stay but the moment you ask any impertinent questions, out you go, do you understand?'

Davies nodded.

'How did you find out where I lived?'

'I, er, used my contacts,' replied the journalist, hoping her answer would satisfy the woman.

After staring at the journalist for a few seconds, Glass nodded.

'Evans, arrange some tea, will you? But don't use the best china.'

The old man nodded and shuffled to the door.

'I don't know why I keep him on, he is really rather past it. So, what do you want, Miss Davies?'

'Well, as you are probably aware, the seventeenth anniversary of the unfortunate fate that befell Miss Sweet, whatever that might have been, is approaching and my editor wants me to do a piece on the event. I wonder, as so many years have passed, whether on reflection, there is anything else you might like to add to what you said at the time?'

'No, why should I? I said everything to the police then, it was all very unfortunate, not quite the thing one expects to happen to one's colleague.'

'Did you work well together?' asked Davies.

Miss Glass glared.

'Careful, Miss Davies,' she said, 'why do you suppose we did not? I didn't always agree with her methods and said so, certainly a new broom and all that but she got things done and all in all was very effective. She was a woman of sound principals and was appreciated by staff and pupils alike and everyone was very upset when she disappeared.'

'Have you ANY idea what might have happened to her?' questioned the journalist.

'No, none but that hasn't stopped me wondering over the years. It was all very sad.'

Some minutes later, Evans appeared at the door bearing a tea tray.

'Tell me, Miss Davies, are the police still involved? You're beginning to sound like a detective in your own right.'

Evans poured the tea.

'Milk and sugar, Miss Davies?'

'Just milk, thank you, Mr Evans. No, as far as I know, they aren't, but if I find something of value, I will of course take it to them.'

'Well, if you do, could you let me in on the secret? I would so like to keep up with developments. I don't yet have a telephone but if necessary you can write a letter or otherwise leave a note with Evans.'

'I'll bear that in mind, Miss Glass.'

'Please do,' the woman replied, 'and I shall be extremely cross if I read any nonsense in your paper as the result of our chat today.'

'Sorry if I got you into trouble,' the journalist whispered as the butler conducted her to the front door at the end of proceedings.

'That's all right, Miss Davies, I'm used to it,' he replied smiling slightly, 'at least you've broken the ice with madam, which helps; her bark is generally worse than her bite.'

Davies almost bumped into her editor as she walked through the office door.

'Well, have you caught up with Miss Glass yet?'

'Yes, Mr Robinson, just got back but didn't learn anything new, she definitely seems to be upset about Miss Sweet's disappearance.'

'How did she strike you?' he asked.

'Oh, a bit domineering, I suppose, used to getting her own way. Admitted to disagreements with Sweet but seemed to accept that the woman had qualities.'

'So, what happens next?'

'I think I'll try Sweet's parents, Mr Robinson.'

'All right, but go easy on them, they must be extremely elderly now if they're still around, keep me informed.'

After some effort, Davies traced the Sweet family to the outskirts of Hereford and, speaking to them on the phone, arranged to see them the next day.

At about ten o'clock the next morning, having travelled over by train and bike, Diana Davies knocked on the door of a small cottage which was opened by an elderly man.

'Miss Davies? Oh, please come in, but I'm not sure that it's a good idea you visiting us.'

'And this is my wife,' said Mr Sweet, introducing a white-haired lady who appeared in the hallway.

'Please go in and sit down, Miss Davies, I was saying to my wife a moment ago that we think this is not a good idea or maybe perhaps it is.'

The journalist looked puzzled.

'I'm sorry but I'm a little confused perhaps I didn't explain myself properly on the phone. All I'm interested in is chatting to you about your late daughter with a view to my paper, properly marking the anniversary of her disappearance.'

The couple exchanged glances.

'This is all rather difficult,' continued the old man, 'what I mean is we didn't quite tell the police everything at the time.'

'Oh,' said Davies, raising an eyebrow, 'what didn't you tell them?'

'Go and get the letter, dear,' said the old man gently.

Mrs Sweet got up and went to a writing desk in the corner of the room, opened the top drawer and returned carrying a sheet of paper. She handed it to the journalist with tears in her eyes.

'I think you'd better read this,' she said.

The sheet was typewritten on good quality paper and read: "I know what you are, it must be you. You know what you have to do."

There was no signature.

The journalist frowned.

'I don't quite know what to say, this is extraordinary,' she said; 'have you any idea who sent it or what it means?'

'No,' they replied in unison.

'Are you saying that you didn't show this to the police at the time? This could be extremely important.'

'Well, yes, we are. When they interviewed us after Dorothy's disappearance, it didn't exist. It arrived through the post about a week or two afterwards, it was forwarded by the school, they probably didn't know what to do with it and it had not been opened. If they found her, we were going to tell the police then, but as time went on with no sign of her we decided not to say anything.'

'Have you any idea why anyone should want to send such a letter to your daughter?'

'No, absolutely no idea at all,' replied Mrs Sweet.

'Have you still got the envelope?' asked Davies.

'Yes, it's in the desk drawer, with an outside one, typed just like the letter and sent to Dorothy at the school via the ordinary post. Perhaps they should have given it to the police then and not sent it on to us but I suppose the school wouldn't necessarily have read it. I do so hope that somebody wasn't wanting to be nasty to Dorothy, that would be awful.'

'Well, I think the best thing to do is put it carefully back in the drawer with both envelopes and leave it until the police contact you,' advised the journalist, 'there might be fingerprints or something. Would you like me to speak to them on your behalf? I know the detective chief inspector at Malvern police station quite well.'

'Oh, yes, please, would you, dear?' said Mrs Sweet; 'we would be so grateful. We know it was silly and that we will probably get into trouble but nothing can bring our daughter back.'

Diana Davies let herself out and returned to Malvern.

'Good for you, Miss Davies,' Robinson commented, 'much as I would like to keep it to ourselves, we'll have to tell the police, but it's getting late so I'd leave it until the morning, another few hours is not going to make any difference. At least we've got something to stick on the front page.'

Chapter 8

That same day during the afternoon, Jimmy Alder, a local man, was walking along the narrow, twisting path above Malvern alongside the disused quarry where he had once sweated day in and day out, one minute preparing explosive to blast the rock, the next wielding a pickaxe until he was fit to drop. The quarry had been worked for many years by Archibald Thurrock and Sons, a long-standing local firm but it had fallen on hard times during the depression and work at the quarry had ceased. The conditions had been terrible and the hours long, but at least it was employment.

But Alder, desperate for a job, had eventually ended up working as a dustman. Now there were rumours that operations at the quarry were about to start up again. But it would not be him on the end of a pickaxe, he was past retirement age, but some local lads would, no doubt, take it on despite the poor wages. On the other hand, new ways of quarrying these days might make the job easier. There had been many such operations in the Malvern Hills over the years, but most had closed, leaving deep scars to become gradually overgrown by stunted trees and any other vegetation that could cling to the steep slopes.

Perspiring despite a chilly unseasonable wind, Alder reached a point near the old explosives hut at the edge of the quarry and looked around. Using a pair of binoculars, he often carried to watch the antics of jackdaws which frequented the rocky quarry sides, he scanned the quarry face opposite him in the hope of seeing them and then, for no particular reason, looked down the slope to his left. Something caught his eye; it was something lodged in a crevice about thirty feet below him. He strained to see what it was and suddenly backed away and ran, stumbling, along the path to his bike.

Detective Inspector John Carlsen sat in his office and reflected upon the world and his part in it. Great Malvern was a curious place, it had its moments but seldom did it figure highly in the pantheon of crime in Worcestershire. He sometimes wondered what life might have been like had his grandfather and father stayed in their native Sweden. In the event they had emigrated and both ended up working as factory hands in Birmingham. But that life was not for John Carlsen. The idea of working in a factory was an anathema to him and he cast around for a more fulfilling job. Whilst walking one day in Birmingham, he espied an advertisement for constables on the notice board of a police station and, straight away, set his mind on joining the police. At nineteen, he had applied not for the Birmingham force but Worcestershire county police, his father having moved to Redditch to work in one of the many factories there manufacturing needles and pins. After training, Carlsen was posted to Malvern as a young constable before eventually returning as a Detective Inspector in CID. A stocky man who occasionally wore spectacles and with greying hair he was often accused of not looking like a detective, an accolade that he considered in some circumstances to be an advantage.

Detective Chief Inspector Harold Martin, Carlsen's immediate senior was older, having served in the army and was already in CID when the detective inspector was in basic training, and had been promoted rather earlier than some others. A somewhat burlier and taller man than the inspector, Martin had a reputation for affability, perhaps more so than his DI. But both men worked well together, an essential factor in the efficient running of a CID office.

Carlsen was suddenly brought back to reality by Detective Sergeant Michael Roberts who tapped on his door.

'Looks like we've got a body, sir,' said the sergeant.

'Oh, where's that then?'

'Up in an old quarry on the hills. The bloke who found it is at the front desk, apparently it's a skeleton stuck down one of the slopes.'

'A skeleton down a slope, God, these things are never simple, are they? All right, we'll take the car and he can show us where it is, but before we go, speak to uniform and ask if we can borrow a couple of PCs. Also get on to the photographic boys at County, we'll need some pretty pictures, and ask some lads from the local rock-climbing group to get up there with their ropes; if there's any scrambling about to be done, they can help. And we'll need the doctor as well, I'll speak to the coroner's officer, all the usual stuff.'

An hour and a half later, a little group of people huddled in the cold at the top of the quarry looking down at a skeleton which lay on the quarry pathway.

'Can't say much at the moment,' the doctor was saying 'but its female and obviously been here a long time. We'll have to see what the pathologist says.'

51

'Do you need me anymore, inspector?' asked Alder eventually, 'this has all been a bit of a shock, like.'

'No, not for now,' said Carlsen, 'we've got your details and eventually we'll need a statement. Thanks for your help, sorry you had your walk spoiled. Oh, who owns the quarry by the way?'

'Jesse Thurrock, I used to work for his old man but he's gone now.'

'Do you know where the son lives?'

'Yes, at the big house in Grange Road.'

At that, and still looking shocked, the man disappeared up the path.

'Well, he won't be coming up here for a while,' commented Roberts wryly.

'No, so we'll have a chat with Thurrock on the way back to the nick, lives in Grange Road, eh? Very nice, must be money in quarrying or at least used to be.'

'What do you think about the position of the skeleton?' said Carlsen, directing his question at the leader of the climbers who was clambering back on to the path, 'it seems odd that it remained undetected for so long, and if it's who I think it is, I helped with the original search.'

'Oh, so you know who it might be do you, inspector?'

'I have an inkling, yes, but I need to check it out before I'm certain.'

'Well,' continued the man, 'it looks as if the body was originally snagged onto a tree under the overhang but the tree eventually rotted and couldn't hold it any longer and the skeleton fell a few more feet and became visible.

Roberts, who was staring at the bones lying at his feet suddenly said, 'What's that stuck in the mud around the left elbow, doctor? It seems to be glinting.'

Doctor Johns poked about with one of his instruments and finally removing the object, handed it to Carlsen.

The inspector turned it over in his hand.

'Seems to be a metal clasp of some sort, possibly silver but it's so tarnished that it's difficult to tell. I wonder how it got there?'

The doctor shrugged.

'That's your department, Mr Carlsen, so unless you want me for anything else, I'm off back to the car before I freeze to death, shouldn't be this cold at this time of the year; I recommend you do likewise,' he said grinning. 'I'll leave my report at the station as usual. Death certified at 3:05 p.m., all right?'

'Many thanks, doctor, and thank you, lads,' said Carlsen, 'help much appreciated, but was there anything down there that possibly might have been a clasp like the one here?'

'No, but we did find these,' said the last one to climb out of the quarry who produced the perished remains of what appeared to be wellington boots and pieces of rubber and placed them on the path.

'That's useful,' said Carlsen, 'they ring a loud bell.'

Photographs having been taken, the undertakers who had been hovering nearby were instructed by the coroner's officer to move the skeleton, which was then placed carefully in a coffin before being carried with some difficulty along the narrow path to a hearse.

'Before we go, Roberts, take a walk around the other side of the quarry,' instructed Carlsen, 'see how visible this rock face below our feet is from over there.'

The sergeant returned a few minutes later, puffing slightly from the exertion, his breath quite distinct in the cool air.

'The path peters out, sir, so when you get to that bramble patch over there, that's as far as you can go, nothing but a rock face in front of you. It's no wonder the body was never spotted, because the path we're standing on is longer than the one opposite so the quarry face under our feet is invisible from over there and there is no other vantage point.'

'All right, let's take a look at that shed along the path, see what's in there.'

The shed about twenty feet square was of wood-built construction but had seen better days. The wooden roof was rotting and some of the side timbers were beginning to spring outwards.

'Probably a relic of the old days,' said Roberts, 'must have used it to store explosives and such like.'

Carlsen opened the door from which hung a broken, rusting hasp and a locked padlock, but apart from a rotting wooden bench and some shelving, the hut was empty.

'Not much in here, sir,' remarked Roberts.

'No, didn't expect to find anything really and nor did we ten years ago. OK, let's go back to the nick and start the paperwork. The guvnor is going to be keen to solve this one once and for all.'

'So, you know quite a bit about our skeleton, sir?'

'Yes, think I do, Roberts, but wait until I've talked to Mr Martin back at the station and I'll explain.'

Back in the office, Carlsen spoke to his DCI.

'I'm going to draw the papers on any missing persons, sir, maybe dental records will help but I've already had an idea about the identity of our body. You weren't here at the time but a young headmistress from the Girls' College, called Sweet suddenly disappeared about seventeen years ago not long after her appointment and hasn't been seen since. So, it's quite likely that the body is hers, especially as a pair of rotten wellies and some rubberised material probably from her mac was found at the bottom of the quarry; they've got to be Sweet's. I helped in the search of the quarry at the time because she was supposed to like to walk up there, but nothing was found, it was all very strange.'

'Yes, I remember, I was a PC over at Kidderminster then, it was the biggest thing that had happened in Malvern for years. Anyway, I'll have a word with the press, they may be able to help. What's that silver thing you've got there?'

'Well, it seems to be a clasp from the handle of a handbag, which would make sense, the other one's probably at the bottom of the quarry somewhere, the climbing lads said there was no sign of it. The likelihood has to be that it's off Dorothy Sweet's handbag if she was carrying one, which is likely; most women have a handbag even if they're only out for a walk. Trouble is trying to prove it came off hers which has probably rotted. Anyway, the lab. boys can take a look at it. I'll have a look at the statements taken at the time to see whether there's any mention. Worcester can also take a gander at the rubber remains of the mac and the wellington boots to confirm that they came from her or, at least, a female.'

'Do you know, I wonder why the body was never spotted at the time of the search if it was only a few feet below the lip of the path?' asked Martin.

'Well, as I recall, it was very overgrown, more so than now, and the body probably fell through bushes or small trees before becoming tangled up. By the time it stopped, it must have been well hidden and Sweet was fairly small and lightly built; still, sounds like an excuse, doesn't it?'

'Yes, but it's not your fault, you weren't in charge of the search. But the question remains, did she just slip and fall or was she pushed? I suppose she could have lain there still alive for hours, poor cow.'

That day late in the afternoon, Martin received a phone call from the home office pathologist.

'Can't do much with the body you sent me, chief inspector, it's been in that quarry too long. The skull is damaged as, no doubt, you noticed at the scene, impossible to say though whether this is the result of an assault beforehand or due to the fall on the rocks but probably the latter. From what you told me, it's quite a long way down there. What I can say is that it's a woman probably in her forties about five feet seven inches tall. If you can let me have the dental records of any likely candidates, then maybe I can be of more help. I will then send you my official report.'

A short time later, Martin called Carlsen to his office.

'I've had a word with the pathologist, there is very little doubt the body is Dorothy Sweet, John, her physical characteristics match up with the information we have. But he needs her dental records to confirm it.'

'That's useful because Roberts has found them at a practice in West Malvern, sir, and I'm having them taken to Worcester.'

'Good, at least her family will be pleased if it's confirmed, or relieved is probably a better word.

'Anyway, you'd better get a squad organised and re-interview the original witnesses. I wouldn't bother with a man called Clover, though, at least not yet, according to the file which Worcester sent us they didn't have much joy with him at the time. He worked at the school, bit of a toerag but nothing could be proved regarding any links with Sweet's disappearance. Speak to the quarry owner, Thurrock, see if he can help. We'd better get it right this time, John, otherwise we might get some clever-dick detective down from the Yard poking his nose in, which will not please the chief constable.'

'I've had a verbal report from Worcester on the clasp, sir,' said the DI, 'doesn't tell us much that we don't know already. Definitely silver, made in Birmingham in 1919, which means it's in a likely time frame for our victim, and definitely off some sort of bag. We could visit Sweet's parents if they're still around, they might be able to identify it. I'll get one of the DCs on to it, their address is bound to be in the file somewhere. Also, Worcester say that the rubber remains are from a mac but can't say whether it was from Sweet or not and likewise the wellies were made for a female.'

The following morning, phone rang in Martin's office.

'Chief Inspector, this is the pathologist, I can confirm that your body out of the quarry is that of Dorothy Sweet, her dental records match exactly.'

Martin thanked him and gave a sigh of relief.

'Well, thank God for that, progress at last.'

Later, Detective Constable Finch knocked on the door.

'Excuse me, sir,' he said, 'I've found the Sweet's address.'

'John, contact them if you can find a number. Give them the latest but tell them that we'd like to visit. On second thoughts, no, we can go over and speak to them later and confirm to their faces that we've found their daughter. At the same time, we can show them that clasp, maybe they can identify it.

Meanwhile,' continued Martin, 'I'll organise a press conference for early this afternoon and we can tell them that we still await confirmation of Sweet's identity, not strictly true but it will be something more or less positive to give to them. And we'd better tell them not to contact her parents until at least we've visited them.'

Later a uniform sergeant tapped on Martin's door.

'Sir, there's a Miss Davies from the Malvern Gazette downstairs, she'd like a word if it's convenient.'

'How the hell did she find out about the body so soon, if that's what it's about?' said Martin, 'we haven't told anyone yet.'

'You know what the press are like, sir, they have their contacts just like we have, shall I bring her up?'

'No, I'll come down.'

'I just want a quick word with you, Mr Martin,' she announced at the front counter. 'Yesterday, I visited Mr and Mrs Sweet, the parents of Dorothy Sweet because we're doing a piece to cover the seventeenth anniversary of her disappearance, and they want to show you a letter which they've had for some years and are worried about; I think it's probably quite important. I haven't got it with me as I assumed that you'd want to speak to them in person and I was a bit concerned about fingerprints. It was a bit too late to contact you when I got back.'

'All right, but I think we'd better discuss this in my office, Miss Davies.'

Once upstairs, the journalist summarised her meeting with the Sweets and the chief inspector explained what had happened.

'Not the headmistress? I don't believe it; what an extraordinary coincidence,' she said.

'Yes, that's who we think it is but it's not confirmed yet. I'd prefer it that you kept it to yourself for the time being, we're holding a press conference at 2 p.m., we've just told your editor. We're actually planning to visit the Sweets once that's finished, although local police have already told them the worst.'

'In that case, I'll wait until later for the details, Mr Martin, but where was she found?'

'Up at Thurrock's quarry.'

'Thurrock's quarry? But I thought, oh, never mind it can wait.'

'As I said, please keep it to yourself until the conference later, miss.'

'Oh, by the way, chief inspector,' called the journalist over her shoulder as she turned to leave, 'I didn't put her there, honest.'

'Go away, Miss Davies, you have a macabre sense of humour, I'll see you at 2 p.m. Thanks for the information on the letter,' said Martin grinning.

'Oh, and just to emphasise, chief inspector, Mr and Mrs Sweet are very worried they're going to get into trouble over keeping the letter.'

'All right, we'll treat them gently.'

Early that afternoon, a crowd of journalists waited impatiently outside the police station, frequently consulting their watches and shuffling their feet in the cold as they waited to be let in. Finally at 2 p.m., Martin and Carlsen convened a press conference and immediately faced a clamour of questions. Martin raised his hands and the room fell silent.

'Right, good afternoon, ladies and gentlemen, a body, or more accurately, a skeleton, was found yesterday up at Thurrock's quarry in the Malvern Hills. The body has yet to be formally identified but we have reason to believe that it is that of Miss Dorothy Sweet who, as you probably know, disappeared almost exactly seventeen years ago. We have informed next of kin and will confirm the pathologist's findings as soon as we receive them. I will let you know when there are further developments.'

A cacophony of further questions greeted this statement.

'Was it murder, chief inspector?' someone asked.

'We're not certain and, as I said, we await the pathologist's report. We're not jumping to conclusions,' replied Martin.

'According to the papers at the time, the quarry was searched, why was the body not found then?' another asked.

'Well, we think it was due to the lie of the land and where we presume the body was at the time of her disappearance. We assume it was hidden in vegetation under an overhang near the hut and became snagged on a tree or bush below the quarry edge. It's difficult, if not impossible, to see the spot from the pathway amongst the summer growth. The path on the other side of the quarry does not extend as far as the hut opposite, so the body couldn't have been seen from there either. It seems likely that the remains fell further down the rock face more recently and therefore became visible from the pathway. Therefore, no blame can be laid at the door of the officers involved in the search in 1920; it was, after all, only a missing person enquiry at that point.

'I should also mention that a silver handbag clasp was found on the deceased which may be of help in positively identifying the remains, although I realise it is a bit of a long shot, so please mention that in your reports and ask for anybody with any information to come forward on that or any aspect of the case. I will arrange a further press conference as necessary. Thank you.'

Ignoring further questions, Martin drew Diana Davies aside.

'I just wanted to thank you again for the information you gave us, we're just going over to the Sweets now.'

'Glad to be of help, chief inspector, it was obviously just a coincidence that you found the body, but I thought it best that you visit them yourself rather than me interfering. My editor wants the paper to run a piece in tomorrow's edition. Have you any objection to me mentioning the letter, which I noticed you didn't comment on?'

'No, we'd rather you left that out for the time being, I don't think it would be fair on her parents, especially as we haven't seen it yet. That's why I made no mention of it at the press conference, so please just print what I announced. I'll let you know about the letter.'

'All right, but can you tip me the wink if you get to the bottom of it?'

'You'll be our first port of call, Miss Davies.'

'Oh, by the way, Mr Martin, I've had a chat with Mr Bowers, who did the original story, he got the impression that Miss Glass and Sweet didn't get on. Just thought I'd mention it. Talking of Miss Glass, she lives at Rose Villa, Como Road if you're looking for an address. No phone though.'

The journalist left the police station intending to return to the office straight away, but on a whim decided to make her way to Thurrock's quarry, never having visited the place. On her arrival some while later and having pushed her bike for much of the way, she left the machine at the top of the road then made her way along the footpath that led past the hut. When she had left the police station, there were sunny skies but a mist had descended over the hills soon after her arrival and she pulled up the collar of her thin coat against a slight drizzle. The hut loomed into view and just outside it scuff marks on the pathway indicated where she assumed the remains of Miss Sweet had been brought up from the rocks below. I wonder whether that might make a good photograph, she pondered. She would mention it to the editor on her return. Davies craned her neck over the edge of the path, but seeing nothing in the gloom, decided to return to the office.

'Can I help you, miss?' said a male voice.

The journalist nearly jumped out of her skin and, spinning around, discovered a man standing there who had approached unheard through the mist.

'Sorry to frighten you,' he replied, 'my name's Jesse Thurrock, I own the quarry.'

'Diana Davies from the Gazette,' she said. 'I thought I'd come up and have a look around.'

'You know about the body then?'

'Yes, I've just been to a press conference at the police station.'

'The police have been in contact and told me what they'd found,' he said, 'couldn't help though. Anyway I won't disturb you any further, good afternoon.'

The man turned on his heal and returned the way he had come.

Back at the Gazette she conferred with her editor.

'It rather gave me the creeps, that place, especially in the mist and I also bumped into the owner but he didn't say much. Anyway, I was wondering whether it might be worth getting a photographer up there, perhaps a picture of the hut and the place where they got the body up? You can see some marks on the pathway.'

'Good idea, I'll arrange it, we can put it on the front page,' replied Robinson, 'by the way, did you see the ghost?'

'And what ghost might that be?' she asked suspiciously to sniggers around the office.

'Well, one of the quarrymen blew himself up sometime around the turn of the century. Some said it was a faulty fuse on a stick of dynamite, others said that he had committed suicide. His ghost is supposed to walk the quarry paths with a piece of fizzing explosive in his hand.'

'I'll bear it in mind on my next visit, Mr Robinson,' she responded laughing.

Meanwhile, Martin and Carlsen drove to Hereford and spoke to Mr and Mrs Sweet who were unable to identify the silver clasp.

'Will we go to prison because of the letter, Mr Martin?' asked Mr Sweet after they had had a talk, 'we've been rather silly.'

'We'll try and make sure you don't,' Martin replied reassuringly.

'Poor old souls,' remarked Carlsen after they had left, 'but the letter's interesting. I can't believe that Dorothy Sweet was bent in any way. From what we know about her, it doesn't make sense; so, what's it all about, I wonder? '

After returning from Hereford Martin, Carlsen and Roberts were to be found in the chief inspector's office examining the letter the couple had provided.

'Well,' Martin said to the detective sergeant, 'what do you make of it?'

Roberts shrugged.

'Typewritten, good quality paper, watermark, no spelling mistakes, grammar's OK. Pity no prints that I can see, might have been if her parents had told us sooner. Question is: who sent it and why?'

'All good questions, but did you notice the typewriter has a problem with the letter "a", sarge?' Carlsen remarked, 'it's slightly askew.'

'Yes, sir, but there must be a million and one of these machines out there and a good many with dodgy letters.'

'Well, one of those is the one we're interested in.'

Roberts looked at the floor and smiled.

'Point taken, so where do we start, sir?'

'Well, we have to consider those closest to Sweet, both personal and professional, so start with the school, what typewriters were in use when Miss Sweet was in charge and who had access to them, teachers and so on. You deal with that, use one of the DCs. I'll get the letter over to County, see what they make of it, there might be something we've missed.'

'Thing is, John,' said Martin. 'What's the letter all about, possibly blackmail as you mentioned or something else? But there must be some link with the business.'

Later that afternoon, Carlsen returned to his office and Roberts joined him.

'Any luck with the typewriter yet, sarge?' Carlsen asked.

'The best reply I can give to that, sir, is, maybe, because all the typewriters in use at the college at the time of Miss Sweet have been replaced, bar one, and it's not the one we want, I had a good look at it. But the good news is that all of them were given to teachers for their own use, and fortunately, Miss Sweet's secretary kept a list of who had 'em. I also managed to get their addresses although the school was a bit reluctant.'

'And?' Carlsen queried.

'Well, there's four on the list,' continued Roberts, producing a piece of paper from his pocket, 'Miss Glass, Sweet's deputy, Miss Reid, the school secretary, now retired but living in Malvern, Miss Plant, one of the gym mistresses, retired to Herefordshire apparently, and a Miss Stubbs, another teacher, she's dead though. But as well as the others, we need to trace her family just to check whether the typewriter still exists. The college don't seem to know where they might be but they're checking.'

'All right, Roberts, contact who you can and see whether we can trace this machine. If we can't find it, we need to think again. Trouble is, we don't know what lay behind the letter being sent in the first place, but no question that the intention was to put the black on the headmistress and it may be connected to her death. It's a good job that Miss Sweet's old folks decided to tell us about it, albeit prompted by our journalist friend.'

'Another point, sir, when I was leaving the college, I was approached by one of the long-serving teachers, a Miss Rawlins, who was working at the place when Sweet was there and Glass was deputy head. Apparently, there was not much love lost between Sweet and Glass although they tried to keep it quiet. It seems that there was a certain amount of jealousy because Glass had applied for the post of headmistress but Sweet was favoured by the governors, also Glass didn't always agree with Sweet's methods. I mean it's not evidence that Glass had anything to do with Sweet's disappearance but it's interesting.'

'Well, that certainly IS interesting,' responded Carlsen, 'that they didn't always get on is mentioned in the case papers and also by our journalist friend so its useful confirmation. I'll mention it to Mr Martin. Well done, Roberts, arrange for her to give a statement, will you?'

The following day, the letter arrived back in Martin's office, "confirmed no distinguishable fingerprints", stated the report.

'Damn,' said DCI Martin but he was hardly surprised.

DS Roberts then appeared at the door.

'I've spoken to Miss Reid,' he said, 'she doesn't have her machine anymore, it broke and was thrown away years ago, no reason to doubt that. I can't trace Miss Plant's address but am working on that. I'm still waiting for the college to ring back with the Stubbs's relatives' address if they can find it. Miss Glass, I see tomorrow.'

'No luck, with dabs on the letter, Roberts, nothing found. Let me know how you get with the Glass woman. Oh, and that journalist, Diana Davies, has been pestering me for information on how we're getting on since she found out about the letter to Miss Sweet. Let her sweat a while otherwise she'll make us all redundant; I reckon she's angling to get on the nationals. But she's good, you have to give her that and she's not as devious as some journalists I've met.'

'Yet, sir,' commented Roberts cynically.

The following morning, the detective sergeant beat a path to Miss Glass's door and having negotiated passage with Evans, who carefully examined his warrant card, ushered him into her presence.

'Well, first the newspapers and now the police, I am having a busy time of it. What can I do for you?'

'Thank you for seeing me, madam,' said Roberts, 'but police are reopening the enquiry into the death of Dorothy Sweet because, as you probably know, her remains have just been found up in that quarry.'

'Yes, I read about it, it's all very sad and just after that journalist came to see me too but you're not likely to get much further than you did before, unless, of course, something more has happened.'

'Well, there has been a development, we're trying to trace a particular typewriter which was used to type a letter which was sent to Miss Sweet at around the time of her death and which has just come to light.'

'Oh, what kind of letter?' She asked, eyes narrowing.

'Well, I don't want to disclose the contents but it was not very pleasant.'

'I hope you're not accusing me, sergeant.'

'We're not accusing anyone at the moment, madam, but do you, by any chance, still have the machine you used at the school? According to an old list, you were offered one when they were all replaced.'

Miss Glass hesitated.

'I'm just trying to remember; I vaguely recall accepting a typewriter but I don't really know whether it's still around.'

There was a long pause.

'Forgive me, madam, but you must know whether you own a typewriter or not,' persisted Roberts, becoming unnecessarily impatient, 'it's important.'

'Don't be impertinent,' she shot back, 'I certainly did have one but having just about retired I've not much need of a machine these days. I'm just trying to remember what happened to it.'

'Sorry, madam, perhaps your butler could help,' suggested Roberts helpfully.

'I'm sure he won't,' she replied.

'Please ask, madam,' said Roberts.

'Evans,' she squawked, 'the officer wants to know what happened to my old typewriter, have you any idea where it is?'

'Why, yes, madam,' replied Evans entering the room, 'it's on the housekeeper's old desk, you may remember you said that should you employ a housekeeper again she might find a typewriter useful in her duties.'

Miss Glass sighed and looked slightly embarrassed.

'Yes, thank you Evans, I suppose you want to look at it, officer?'

'If that's convenient, madam.'

'Well, if that's all, Evans can show it to you on the way out.'

'Thank you, madam, that's all I require.'

'Well, I hope none of this gets into the press, I suppose you'll be telling them all about my typewriter.'

'We will not tell the press anything, madam,' said Roberts.

'Maybe not but they have a habit of finding out about these things,' she countered, 'if they do, I shall hold you fully responsible.'

Ignoring the remark but muttering his thanks, Roberts accompanied Evans to the housekeeper's room, and inserting a piece of paper into the dusty machine, typed a few words. After a few seconds, Roberts shook his head.

'Well, you can tell Miss Glass that this is not the one, Mr Evans,' said Roberts, 'there'll be no need to take it away. Has she ever owned another machine to your knowledge?'

'Not in my time, Sergeant Roberts, and I've been with her for some years, heaven help me.'

'All right, thanks. We'll be in touch again if we need to.'

Back at the station, Roberts passed on the news to his DI.

'Nothing doing, sir, as regards Glass's machine, definitely not the same one, and the butler says it's the only one she's ever owned. Could have used another typewriter which we don't know about, I suppose.'

'Yes unfortunately. But what was Glass's reaction?'

'Oh, a bit starchy, worried about it getting in the press.'

'Well, that leaves the dead Miss Stubbs and her family, if any, Miss Reid and Miss Plant, you try and contact her and Stubbs's family, and I'll see if I can speak to the Reid woman. See if we can speed things up a bit; if it turns out to be a dead end, we've got some more thinking to do.'

Carlsen conferred with Martin over a cup of tea the following morning.

'No luck with the typewriter angle, sir, the only ones we haven't examined yet are the ones given to the late Miss Stubbs and the one belonging to Plant which Roberts has tried to follow up but with no luck. Apparently, the Stubbs family lives or lived in Herefordshire but no address, so we might have to resort to voters' registers for her and the others.'

'Well, I think we need to see those typewriters, John, if no other reason than elimination. It's desperation stakes at the moment. Oh, and any response to the piece in the Gazette regarding witnesses by the way?'

'No, not yet, sir, but the paper only came out late yesterday afternoon so there's time yet.'

'Either way, we're struggling a bit. All we have is a letter and there's no clue as to who sent it or why and a silver clasp which the Sweets can't identify. It's only a matter of time before old Fowler comes over from County demanding to know what's happening; I need something positive to tell him.'

'I'll keep at it, sir.'

Carlsen then called DS Roberts to his office.

'Even if we can't find the other machine, we seem to have a better chance of tracing the machine that Stubbs used. Try and trace her family in the voters' lists at Hereford and then pay a visit. The guvnor's getting anxious, wants to cover all the angles.'

Later that day, Roberts reported progress.

'Just got back from Hereford, sir, found the Stubbs' address in the voters and I've got the typewriter on my desk; fortunately, the family kept it. I haven't tried it out yet but it definitely looks to have a dodgy "a".'

Both men went into the CID office and examined the machine, with Roberts inserting a piece of paper.

'See that "a", sir, it's out of alignment and this proves it; it's the same as on the letter.'

'Good,' responded the DI, 'now we're getting somewhere, except of course Stubbs is dead. We'd better check her out anyway. Go back to the school if you have to, we need to know about her relationship with Miss Sweet, and see whether there was any possible reason to send that letter.'

'Well, I spoke to her surviving sister, sir, apparently Stubbs was quite an amiable type, wouldn't hurt a fly but you never know, she might have been totally different when working at the school. In any case, it doesn't necessarily follow that she had sole access to the machine the letter could have been typed by anyone before the old typewriters were redistributed.'

'I agree, and I don't think we need to waste any more time on the Reid typewriter, Roberts, as things stand at the moment, we have to establish whether it was likely that the Stubbs woman sent the letter and why.'

Chapter 9

It was the middle of the evening in late October 1937 and Constable Grimes looked at his watch twice and then sighed. There were still a few hours to go before he was due to finish late turn. It was getting dark and the streetlights were gradually coming on one by one along Graham Road. There was drizzle in the air, it was suddenly chilly and he pulled his cape around him. As he passed "The Camelias", a frenzied but muffled shout suddenly erupted from somewhere on the top floor of the house.

'Help me, someone, please help me,' said a female voice.

Grimes stared through the gloom at a single light which burned on the top floor as a figure struggled to open a window. He hurried to the front door but it was shut fast, however, running around to the back of the house, there was an open door and finding the hallway ran up the stairs as a woman's voice continued to shout for help. He noticed that blood was spattered liberally on the wall at the side of the stairs, the bannisters and the stair carpet.

'It's the police, where are you?' Grimes called from the top of the stairs.

'I'm here, I'm here,' replied a woman, who suddenly burst out of one of the doors practically knocking the constable off his feet.

'It's terrible, it's awful,' she cried hysterically.

'What's happened here?'

'In there, in there, she's in there,' the woman replied, gesticulating wildly towards a door.

'Stay here,' instructed Grimes, who then entered the room.

Lying on the bedroom floor by the window was what appeared to be a middle-aged woman, her features almost unrecognisable. A large pool of blood was soaking into the carpet and a broken vase lay nearby. She was clearly dead.

'Have you a phone?' said the constable, racing down the stairs in anticipation.

'Yes, on the left at the bottom of the stairs,' gulped the woman.

Five or so minutes later, an ambulance drew into the drive but an ambulance man soon emerged from the bedroom shaking his head, his hands covered in blood.

'Sorry, mate, too late, she's gone,' he was saying, 'I can't take her, you'd better get your doctor to take a look, she's definitely a candidate for the mortuary.'

DI Carlsen arrived some minutes later and raced up the stairs, meeting Grimes at the top.

'There's a dead woman in the bedroom, sir, she's had her skull bashed in but I don't who she is yet, I haven't had a chance to ask. This lady here is the one who found her, she's had a terrible shock.'

'Wait here, please,' said Carlsen to the woman. He then went in and examined the body before consulting with the ambulance men.

'Grimes,' he ordered, 'get onto the nick, use the phone at the bottom of the stairs, speak to DCI Martin and explain what's happened, he wasn't there when I left but if he's not back arrange to get a message to him in the CID car. Plus, I want the police doctor up here, the coroner's officer, the fingerprint blokes from County and a photographer, plus any DCs that may have returned to the office. Tell me when you've done it and then stand on the door and stop anyone you don't know from coming in, got it? Oh, and I also want any spare uniform constables available.'

'Yes, sir.'

'Who are you, madam, please?' Carlsen asked the woman, who was shaking and weeping nearby.

'I'm, I'm Miss Adams's housekeeper, Mrs Black, I come in every day, I couldn't get a reply so I came upstairs and then I found her in the bedroom. Who could have done such a thing? It's terrible, I'll never get over it.'

'Miss Adams, you say.'

'Yes, Miss Olive Adams, I've been coming here for years, I usually pop in at this time of the evening to see if she's all right before she goes to bed.'

'How did you get in then?'

'By the back door, she always leaves it open during the day.'

'Did you seen anyone at all leaving the house or hurrying along the street?'

'No, not that I noticed.'

'Can you think of any reason why anybody would want to harm her?'

'No.'

' Is she married, Mrs Black ?'

' No.'

'Who is her next of kin, do you know?'

'She's got a sister but I don't know where she lives.'

'Have you a name by any chance?'

'Esther or Ethel, some name like that I think.'

'Is this sister married?'

'No, I don't think so.'

'Is there anything obvious missing as far as you can see?'

'No.'

'All right, thank you, that will do for the moment, Mrs Black, we'll need a statement from you eventually, but for now I'll get one of my officers to accompany you home when one arrives. Is there somebody there who can be with you?'

'Yes, my husband.'

'Excuse me, sir,' interrupted Grimes, 'Mr Martin is on his way and he is speaking to County.'

'All right, good.'

'Fill me in, John,' said a voice a few minutes later, 'I got your message and have done the necessary with Worcester.'

DCI Martin followed by DS Roberts, DC Grover and several uniform officers, was mounting the stairs.

'A lady called Olive Adams, has had her skull smashed in, sir. Mrs Black, her housekeeper found her, so needless to say, very upset. She's downstairs, waiting for someone to accompany her home; a PC can go with her, apparently she doesn't live far.

'PC Richards, arrange to go with Mrs Black please, and stay with her if her husband's not there,' said Carlsen.

'Have we any suspects, John?'

'No, not yet, sir, I've had a brief word with Mrs Black, not much help yet, didn't see anything. I'll get Roberts and Grover to set the ball rolling on door to door. They can do the immediate local stuff tonight but we're going to need some DCs from Worcester to help with legwork with Roberts in charge, perhaps you can speak to Mr Fowler about that?'

'Yep, I'll get on the blower back at the nick, at least I'll have something to tell him but probably not what he wants to hear,' said Martin. 'Poor old soul, what did she do to deserve this?'

'Right, someone is wandering about with possibly an awful lot of blood on them, sir, I'll get on the radio and put out an "all cars".'

The chief inspector then went into the bedroom and examined the body before emerging to the sound of voices a few minutes later.

'We meet again. Evening, chief inspector, what have you got for me then?' asked Rogers, the police doctor who was puffing up the stairs. 'Bit of a mess, eh?'

'That's only the half of it, doctor, she's in there.'

Rogers emerged about five minutes later, his hands bloody.

'Been dead no more than an hour to an hour and a half, I would say, minimal rigor mortis, obviously had her skull smashed in by that vase. Pity that, a valuable piece of Japanese Imari, I would say, too far gone to be restored, oh well.'

Martin's eyes shot skywards.

'A bit mercenary, Doctor Rogers,' commented Martin.

The man smiled thinly.

'Got to lighten the atmosphere in this game a bit, chief inspector, otherwise it would drive you mad, you must know that by now. Where's the bathroom please? I'll try not to touch anything.'

'Hm, I suppose you've got a point,' conceded the DCI.

'Before I finish, the woman also seems to have been stabbed as well as being clobbered with that vase. There are a number of shallow stab wounds on her right side and also in the upper back, suggesting that she might have run upstairs while being pursued by her attacker. But they, on their own, wouldn't have been enough to kill her. Used a knife with a short blade curved at the end, I imagine, no sign of it anywhere, I suppose? Certified death, say 8:30 p.m.,' said the doctor, glancing at his watch. 'Anyhow, I'll let you have my report as soon as I can, but I think the pathologist will want to come over before you move the body. I'll try and contact him; may I use the phone? Trouble is, he's probably got his feet up with a gin and tonic by now, lucky devil.'

'Right, John, once the pathologist and the other blokes from County have done their bit, we'll get the body moved and close the place up once we've had a good look around. The coroner will also have to be told and we'll need at least one PC in the drive overnight and more in the morning to fend off the press and anybody else. Thing is, who on earth would want to kill her, burglary gone wrong maybe?'

Carlsen shrugged.

'Possibly, but nothing obvious missing at the moment, sir, but we'll have to check that out with her sister if we can find her.'

'We'll speak to the housekeeper tomorrow,' continued Martin, 'she may feel more like talking to us then, and also I want a thorough search of the garden in daylight to see if we can find this knife and also neighbouring gardens, street side vegetation, rubbish bins etc. Just in case our murderer dumped it somewhere. Roberts can assist with that.'

'Yes, sir, I'll organise it.'

'Also, John, I want to know all about the victim; background, friends etc. Anyone she might have fallen out with enough to be murdered.'

The pathologist eventually appeared and introduced himself.

'Good evening, officer,' he said, 'is it as messy in there as it is out here?'

'I'm afraid so, sir.'

Ten minutes later, the pathologist emerged.

'As Doctor Rogers said, "head bashed in and a few minor stab wounds". But whoever hit her did so with tremendous force. I'll telephone you later tomorrow with my preliminary findings and send you my official report in due course. You can get the body moved now, chief inspector, I'll have a proper look at her on the slab in the morning.'

'What about dabs, anything significant?' enquired Martin of the Worcester men who were preparing to leave.

'Yes, sir,' replied one, 'prints mixed with blood on the vase. We'll see if they can be identified but most are very smudged, looks as if the suspect attempted to rub them off. However, there are a couple of clear marks on the base not tainted with blood. Anyway, we'll take all the bits to Worcester and have a closer look.'

'Any identifiable prints with blood on them elsewhere in the house on the staircase and wallpaper?' the DCI continued. 'Again, there seem to be some smudged marks.'

'Yes, sir, several on the wallpaper in the bedroom as well as the bannisters and wall and also a couple of bloody ones on the doorpost of the back door, our suspect presumably left that way.'

'Good, let me know as soon as you can confirm anything on the dabs. All right, let's get the body moved.'

Early the following morning after a late night, Martin and Carlsen held a conference in the chief inspector's office.

'I've spoken to Mr Fowler,' the chief inspector was saying, 'and he's agreed to help out with manpower; he's coming over this morning, heaven help us. Try Mrs Black again as soon as you can, John, she might remember something. We also might have to use her for formal identification if we can't trace a relative; she's going to love that.'

Soon enough, the detective superintendent was sitting in Martin's office.

'Well, what's doing with this murder, Mr Martin?'

'No witnesses, no motive yet, sir, elderly lady lived by herself, daily visit by a housekeeper, head bashed in sometime late yesterday and there's also a knife involved. We're still looking for that and I'm waiting for a call from the pathologist to fill in the details. There are a couple of clear dabs on the base of the murder weapon, a vase, but possibly they belong to the victim or her housekeeper.'

'Good, I've organised some help from Worcester,' continued Fowler, 'they should be arriving any time now. Keep them as long you need to.'

'I know you've got your hands full, but what about the Sweet case, anything more on that?'

'No, sir, no idea yet as to why she ended up in that quarry.'

'Well, you'd best get your skates on, chief inspector, before my guvnor starts knocking on my door. If he comes a visiting, my next port of call will be you.'

'Understood, sir.'

'Yes, well keep me abreast of developments, anywhere I can get a decent pint?'

Later, the chief inspector was to be found sitting glumly in his office as Carlsen walked in.

'You look as you've lost a quid and found sixpence, sir.'

'I've just had a visit from Mr Fowler, says he's going to jump on me from a great height if we don't make progress on the Sweet business as well as this murder. Still, that's my problem, but to keep him sweet I promised to buy him a pint or maybe two sometime to keep him happy. Any sign of those DCs from Worcester yet?'

'Should be here shortly, Roberts can sort out who is going where. I think we need to cover the whole of Graham Road and the side roads as soon as possible. I'll go up there from time to time to keep an eye on things. We've got some PCs on the door up at the Adams house and I'm going to look through the woman's papers to see if we can trace her sister's address. Roberts is organising a search of the garden and those in the vicinity for this knife we're after and also litter bins in the area. I'll also get on to the council just in case the dustmen come across it.'

'Yes, all right, there are already several press hanging around up there, I'll hold a conference early this afternoon and try to keep them at bay for a little while.'

Just before the appointed time, there was a familiar voice.

'Good afternoon and how are you, chief inspector?'

It was Diana Davies.

'Oh, overworked and underpaid as usual, Miss Davies, how's the world of journalism?'

'Well, it's a job and I'd quite like to keep it, so I hope you've got something to tell me,' she replied.

'As usual, we're seeking the help of the great British public and the ladies and gentlemen of the press,' replied Martin, 'I'll see you at the conference in a minute, and in connection with the Sweet business, you can use the letter in your articles if you wish. Mr and Mrs Sweet are quite happy if it's going to help the investigation.'

'OK, thanks.'

'I'll answer any questions as we go along,' said Martin as he addressed the throng, 'but an elderly lady at an address in Graham Road has been murdered, we believe yesterday evening. We can't yet confirm the identity of the victim as next of kin have not yet been informed. A blunt instrument was used in the crime but we're also looking for a knife, probably one with a short, curved blade and likely to be bloodstained. If anyone should find it, don't touch it but please contact us.

'In addition, whoever was responsible would have had considerable bloodstaining on their clothing, so it's hard to believe that somebody didn't see something.'

Davies put up her hand.

'Do you think the murder of this woman is linked with the death of Miss Sweet?'

The chief inspector looked surprised.

'No, there is no evidence of that.'

'Also a while ago,' she continued, 'you were looking at typewriters in the hope of tracing a letter that was sent to Miss Sweet before her death, have you had any luck tracing who sent it?'

'No, that's come to a dead end at the moment but we're still looking into it. The letter was obviously sent for a reason but we don't yet know why. So, the case is still open and we continue to look for answers, and even after all this time if there's anyone with information who can help, please speak to us no matter how insignificant it might appear.'

'No luck with the knife, sir,' reported DS Roberts to Carlsen later that day after the press conference had, at last, finished. A couple of DCs and myself have had a good look around the garden at the murder scene and also nearby properties, which caused a bit of bellyaching from the neighbours. Nothing found so far on the roadsides or in the litter bins either.'

'Thanks, sarge, well at least we tried, our murderer obviously still has it or has dumped it somewhere else. I mentioned it at the press conference so, hopefully, that will produce something but I'm not counting on it. We might have to extend the search area back towards the town and if necessary the other way to the Common but I'll have to speak to Mr Martin about that. We may need a lot more manpower.'

The phone rang in Martin's empty office as Carlsen was speaking. It was the pathologist with a preliminary report.

'Nothing unexpected, sir,' Carlsen reported to the chief inspector who appeared later, 'the pathologist has confirmed that it was a short-bladed knife, curved at the end giving a distinctive shape. Problem is where the hell is it?'

The following afternoon, the DCI received an unexpected phone call.

'My name is Miss Stephanie Smith,' said a voice, 'I was the headmistress at Bushley School near Queenhill on the other side of Upton, I've heard through the grapevine of the awful murder of Olive Adams. I think I ought to talk to you, may I come over now?'

'Yes, of course, Miss Smith,' replied Martin, somewhat taken aback, 'or if you prefer I can visit you?'

'No, that won't be necessary, I'll be there in about twenty minutes, goodbye.'

'John, my office please.'

Martin explained the situation.

'Perhaps she's going to confess to both murders, sir,' said Carlsen, more in hope than expectation.

'If only police work was that straight forward, John.'

The two had just finished a cup of tea when Sergeant White appeared at the office door.

'A Miss Smith to see you, sir, she's downstairs in the waiting room.'

'Good, show her up.'

'Thanks for coming in, Miss Smith,' said Martin as the former headmistress entered his office, 'I'm Detective Chief Inspector Martin, the officer in the case. This is my colleague, Detective Inspector Carlsen. I believe you may be able to help us regarding the murder of Olive Adams?'

'Well, I hope so, it may be nothing but I think you should know. I received a visit at my school many years ago from someone who was enquiring about the whereabouts of Olive Adams and it was all rather unpleasant.'

'Unpleasant?'

'Yes, I'm afraid so, it was a woman called Leticia Glass. She was a teacher at the Abbey School.'

'Oh, we know this woman, what happened?'

'Well, I can't remember her precise words, it was such a long time ago, but she wanted to know where the murdered lady lived because of something that happened long ago at a school in Herefordshire where we were all pupils. And not only Olive Adams, there were two other girls who were involved in the incident, a Margaret Cameron and Fiona Clerk. I denied that I knew where Olive lived but I phoned her after Leticia had left to tell her about what had been said and to warn her to be on her guard. Both Margaret and Fiona are dead by the way.'

'What happened at Cherrywood school that so upset Miss Glass?'

The headmistress explained.

'Yes,' responded Martin after she had finished, 'I can see why Miss Glass was annoyed, but why on earth should anyone want to dredge up something that happened in their school days?'

'My sentiments exactly, chief inspector, but Leticia is a strange woman, she never forgets slights, imagined or otherwise, no matter how much time has passed.'

'Well, if Miss Glass did have anything to do with it, she left it an awful long time before exacting revenge. Tell me, what was Miss Adams response to your phone call?'

'Annoyed, not with me but Leticia, although a couple of days later, she contacted me again to say that she had met up with Leticia on the organising committee of the Malvern Festival and that everything was more or less OK.'

'But did Miss Adams mention any subsequent incidents that occurred after contact had been re-established?'

'No, she didn't mention anything, just that they had discussed the Cherrywood business and that things seem to have calmed down.'

'Did you speak to Miss Adams again?'

'No, we weren't particularly close, even though she was only in Malvern. We've exchanged Christmas cards, that sort of thing but we never actually visited each other.'

'And what about Margaret Cameron, did you have any contact with her prior to her death?'

'No, before my conversation with Leticia, I discovered that Margaret had died, she was working out in the Far East a few years ago and caught cholera.'

'And what about Fiona Clerk?'

'I don't know what happened to her, I just heard about her death on the grapevine.'

'Have you spoken to Miss Glass since her visit to you at Bushley?'

'Only in relation to the local schools programme, which was something organised by the headmistress of Abbey School, Miss Brown, where Leticia taught. After the contretemps in my study, we've tended to avoid each other. Certainly, the subject has never come up again. I'm led to understand that Leticia has retired as indeed I have, so our paths are not likely to cross again. But there is something else.

'Oh, yes.'

'Not long after Leticia made the unwelcome visit to my school, I received a letter from her. This letter.' The woman produced an envelope from her handbag.

It read: "Having met you at Bushley yesterday, I have come to the conclusion that you were most unhelpful in my quite reasonable quest for justice and that, accordingly, I will make every effort to make life as uncomfortable for you as I possibly can. I care not a jot whether you speak to Miss Brown or not, that is quite irrelevant. If I remain at the school, I will be nice as pie when circumstances at the meetings dictate but, beware, things will not be as they seem."

'This is extraordinary, Miss Smith,' commented the DCI. Did you speak to Miss Brown about this or even the police?'

'No, I realise I should have done, and in fact I was on the point of ringing her and the police when I got this call from Olive Adams saying that things had calmed down.

'I know I shouldn't have allowed her to get away with it but I have a certain sympathy with her, she is clearly somewhat unhinged and what good would it have done had she been dismissed?'

'And did anything result from the letter?' asked Martin.

'No, thank goodness.'

'All right, does this business still concern you? I mean do you feel threatened?'

'Not so much now, well, of course, I did at first but both of us are retired and I have moved home although I'm still local and it's doubtful that she would actually do anything serious even if she finds out where I live. We mustn't forget that this was many years ago, even allowing for long-term spite.'

'All right, but in the unlikely event that she should she turn up at your home or you otherwise fell threatened, please speak to us.

'And we'll need to keep the letter, which presumably Miss Adams was not aware of ?'

'No, I didn't tell Olive, I thought it might worry her. And thank you for your concern.'

'We mustn't jump to conclusions, Miss Smith,' continued the chief inspector, 'but in the event of a court case, your information may be very relevant. I hope you're prepared to give evidence if necessary?'

'Well, yes, if I have to, but I wouldn't want Leticia or you to think that I am accusing her of murder.'

'No, of course not, but as long as you're aware that we may ask you for help.'

'I understand.'

'Another thing, Miss Smith, we know Olive Adams had a sister and we're trying to contact her as, presumably, she's her next-of-kin. Do you know where we might find her as the coroner needs to know?'

'No, not precisely, as I say, we weren't close but I think it's somewhere in the Leominster area but I don't know her name. But like Olive, I think she's unmarried.'

'You have provided us with a lot of information, Miss Smith,' said the DCI, 'but we'll need a statement from you which we can take now if that's convenient; I'm afraid this job is all about paperwork.'

'Yes, all right that's fine,' she replied.

After that had been completed, Martin rose from his chair and conducted the woman downstairs.

'Thank you for coming, I hope we won't need to trouble you again.'

The former headmistress nodded and left.

'Well, what do you make of it, John?' Martin asked.

Carlsen shook his head, chin resting on his left hand, looking somewhat downcast.

'I don't know, sir, I really don't know, not much to go on, is it? It doesn't really change things much. But Glass is crackers, that's for certain, ought to be in Powick.'

'Yes, but it's hardly evidence of her being responsible for Adams's death, I agree, but Glass certainly has a screw loose so we need to have another chat with the good Leticia. She's all we've got, so we must hope that any usable dabs at the house conveniently turn out to be hers. But before we speak to her, we need to see whether local enquiries come up with anything.

'Interestingly though, the dear Miss Glass is clearly not one to cross,' it seems, and these nuggets of information may come in extremely useful. And, certainly, if we're looking for supporting evidence at court, Stephanie Smith could be our saviour.'

At about four o'clock that afternoon, DS Roberts appeared at Carlsen's door.

'Had a bit of luck on this Adams business, sir, someone who lives in Graham Road reckoned he saw a car, possibly driven by a woman, entering the drive of Adams's house some hours before the body was discovered. Reckons that he remembers it because of damage to the nearside front wing, says it was a black or dark blue Morris, one of the bigger ones. Didn't see it leave though and didn't notice the registration mark. And there's one other thing, DC Fletcher, on loan from Worcester, talked to a neighbour who said he had seen someone, a male, he described as 'official looking' who walked into Adams's drive sometime during the afternoon. Wasn't seen to leave though.'

'Official looking?' queried Carlsen. 'What does that mean?'

'Well, certainly not in uniform, sir, but tallish and fairly well built. Could have been a copper, I suppose. The witness said he might be able to recognise him again but the trouble is he's a bit of an elderly gent and it was some way off, so not sure we can rely on him. And that's about it, sir, we've just about finished enquiries in the immediate vicinity, shall I release the DCs from Worcester?'

'Well done, sarge. Yes, all right, once they've completed the information sheets. We can always expand our enquiries as necessary, now we must find that damaged Morris ASAP; I wonder if Miss Glass owns one? Also, we still need to contact the woman's next of kin, apparently there's possibly an unmarried sister in the Leominster area. Get on to it, will you? We need to get the woman's body formally identified. Oh, and check around the nicks in the county, see if any of their CID visited Adams's address on the day of the murder; if so, what were they up to?' If you have any problems with their guvnors, I'll speak to them. Better get our people to check their diaries as well.'

'Yes, sir, by the way, not yet had a chance to chase up information on Miss Stubbs and her ownership of the typewriter.'

'OK but let me know as soon as possible if there's anything of interest.'

'Next step on Adams, John? the DCI asked, having just appeared.

Carlsen relayed to Martin what Roberts had said.

'Well, that's something, but I wonder what the witness meant about this "official looking person." Who could that be? I think we'll pay the Glass woman a little visit as soon as we hear from Worcester regarding the dabs, and have a look at her car. She'll probably scream to the rooftops about it but there we are.'

The phone interrupted their conversation.

The chief inspector listened intently then, with brief thanks, put the receiver down.

'No luck with the prints, John, they're too smudged apparently, they think the murderer was wearing gloves, possibly linen. Only one or two clear prints but there are no matches in the records, in any case they could well belong to Adams or the housekeeper, so we'll need some elimination prints from them both. The dabs from the gloves are very bloodstained and so badly smudged that they can't be used. Nothing unusual regarding the size of the dabs either, so theoretically it could be a female murderer, which of course would fit. Still, the outcome was to be expected, nothing is ever that straight forward.'

'Nevertheless, sir, we still need to have a chat with Glass as soon as possible.'

'OK, but now the fingerprints have gone against us I don't think we can drag her down the nick unless she puts her hands up to it,' rejoined Martin, 'but we'll see what she has to say about the letter to Stephanie Smith.'

'Agreed.'

The following morning, DCI Martin, DI Carlsen and DC Robins knocked on the door of "Rose Villa" in Como Road. A black Morris fourteen car was parked in the drive.

'Yes, sir, may I help you?' enquired the butler.

'Yes, we're from Malvern police, is Miss Glass available please?'

'One moment, I shall enquire.'

'What?' a female voice shouted in the background. 'What?' she repeated but louder, 'let me speak to them.'

A woman soon appeared at the front door, thrusting Evans aside.

'What do you want?'

'I'm Detective Chief Inspector Martin from Malvern police, and these are Detective Inspector Carlsen and Detective Constable Robins. As you may be aware, a Miss Olive Adams has recently been murdered and we understand that you knew her.'

'Yes, what of it?' she replied suspiciously.

'Well, madam, we wonder whether you might spare us a few minutes to talk about the lady?'

Miss Glass grimaced.

'All right, if you must but I'm a busy woman,' she replied.

Having conducted them to the drawing room, Glass waved them to a seat.

'Thank you for seeing us, madam, how long had you known Miss Adams?' Martin enquired.

'We were at school together.'

'Where was that?'

'Cherrywood in Herefordshire.'

'We understand that there was an incident at the school involving you, a Miss Cameron, Miss Adams, Miss Smith and another girl, Fiona Clerk, who was pushed down the stairs.

'How did you know about that? It's none of your business.'

'We've received some information that suggests that the incident rankled with you to such a degree that you decided to find out where these women lived and impose some sort of punishment. Is that so?'

'I think you had better be very careful where this conversation is taking you, chief inspector. If you're suggesting that I wanted to find this woman in order to murder her, you're completely wrong.'

'If that's the case why did you make a special visit to Miss Smith, the headmistress of Bushley school?'

'Ah, now I understand,' said Leticia Glass, 'you've been speaking to that stupid woman and she's started pointing the finger.'

'Miss Smith has spoken to us, yes, but I repeat, why did you deem it necessary to pay such a visit, which apparently ended so acrimoniously?'

'I merely wished to know whether Stephanie knew of Olive's and Margaret's whereabouts and possibly that of Fiona Clerk who might have been able to clarify things.'

'At the risk of becoming repetitive, why?' persisted the chief inspector.

Leticia Glass sighed.

'All right, yes, I did want to see them about the Cherrywood incident but merely to express my anger at what had happened, not to do them any harm.'

'Even after all the time that had passed, Miss Glass?'

'Yes, because potentially they ruined my career in the teaching profession.'

'So, Miss Smith being unable to supply Miss Adams's and Miss Cameron's address, who apparently is dead anyway as is Miss Clerk, what did you then do to try and find Olive Adams?'

'Nothing, because I decided after considerable agonising that it would be sensible to calm down a little. We, that is Olive and I, met by accident when I was co-opted on to the Malvern Festival organising committee last year, of which she was already a member. I had no idea that she was even living in Malvern, let alone just along Graham Road.'

'So, who recognised who at this committee meeting?'

'I did, I couldn't believe my eyes when she appeared.'

'So, did you have a conversation with her?'

'Only a very brief one.'

'About what?'

'Not Cherrywood, we exchanged some inanities about meeting again after all these years and that was about it.'

'Did you see her again after that?'

'Yes, occasionally.'

'Did you discuss Cherrywood?'

'Once when I gave her a lift home.'

'And who raised the subject?'

'I did and I made it quite clear that I was still very angry at what she and the others had done, despite the passage of time.'

'And what did Miss Adams have to say?'

'Well, she was somewhat mortified and apologetic. Said that she still felt awful about what had happened and wished she could change things.'

'And what was your reaction to that?'

'I decided to accept her apology, against my better judgement.'

'Did you threaten her in any way, Miss Glass?'

'No, I did not.'

'Are you certain about that?'

Leticia Glass, having been relatively calm up to that point, snapped back.

'I've just told you I did not, I warned you earlier on about the direction this conversation was taking. This interview is terminated.'

'Evans,' she squealed, 'show these gentlemen out.'

'No, Miss Glass, I've not yet finished,' said Martin.

'I said this interview is at an end, I wish to speak to my solicitor, I will answer no more of your ridiculous questions.'

'Then we will wait outside until your solicitor arrives, madam, but one way or another, you will answer my questions. If necessary, down at the police station and then it will all be over the press and I'm sure you wouldn't want that, Miss Glass.'

'Get out, get out of my house while I phone my adviser,' she screamed.

After some delay, a car drew up at the front door, disgorging a small, nervous looking man clutching a briefcase. The group who had been waiting in the road approached him.

'I'm Detective Chief Inspector Martin of Malvern police and these are my colleagues,' he said, producing a warrant card, 'are you Miss Glass's solicitor?'

'Yes, I'm Stevens from Worple and Stevens, Priory Road, my client is rather upset, chief inspector, what have you been asking her?'

Martin explained.

'Well, I'll go in and will try to calm her down, I trust there's no possibility of arrest?'

'That depends on the answers to our questions. It is, after all, a murder enquiry,' replied the DCI.

'Wait here, please,' instructed the solicitor.

Five minutes later, the man emerged.

'I have persuaded her to agree to further questioning, Mr Martin, I emphasised that you were merely trying to get to the bottom of a rather unpleasant murder. Nevertheless, I would be obliged if you don't pressure her too much, she claims to be rather unwell and, in any case, ahem, she can be rather difficult.'

'Yes, Mr Stevens, we noticed. I should point out to you that before we resume our conversation with Miss Glass, we propose asking about a letter, a copy of which I will give you now which relates to her relationship with Miss Stephanie Smith, a former headmistress of Bushley school.'

The solicitor examined it carefully.

'Oh, dear, please allow me to have a further word with my client.'

A few minutes later, he emerged and waved them into the house.

Leticia Glass lay in wait with a sour look on her face.

'As I think Mr Stevens has just mentioned to you, can you explain the contents this letter which was given us by Miss Smith?' continued the chief inspector.

Glass glanced at Stevens and then at a copy of the document which lay in front of her.

'It was intended to put pressure on Stephanie, nothing more than that,' she replied after reading it.

'The letter was threatening in tone, Miss Glass, what else did you intend to do?'

'Nothing, I'm telling you, nothing.'

'So you say, but how do we know that you didn't intend to bestow the kind of treatment on Miss Smith as was meted out to Olive Adams?'

'Because I'm telling you, I didn't. I know it was rather stupid but Stephanie Smith made me very angry and I wasn't thinking straight.'

'All right, to continue the question of your treatment of Miss Adams, Miss Glass, did you threaten her at any time?' said Martin.

'That is the third time you've asked me that. No, I did not.'

'What about your car, Miss Glass, is that your Morris fourteen parked outside?'

'Yes.'

'Is it damaged in any way?'

'Yes, the front nearside wing is rather bent; I hit my gatepost with it.'

'When was that?'

'About two months ago. Look, where is all this leading?' Glass demanded.

'A black Morris with a damaged wing was seen entering the driveway of Miss Adams's house, we believe, sometime before the murder.'

'What of it? I gave her a lift on the day of her murder and no, for the final time, I didn't do it and I didn't see any thugs or anyone suspicious hanging around. Now, is that all?'

'Not quite, did Miss Adams seem worried about anything?'

'No.'

'Did you go into her house when you gave her a lift?'

'No, I just dropped her off in the drive.'

'About what time was that?'

'Around 4:30 p.m., I suppose, our meetings usually finish at about a quarter past.'

'Incidentally, does anyone else drive your car, Miss Glass?'

'No.'

'All right, but we need to examine the vehicle if you don't mind and then we'll be finished.'

'If you must, but I want you present, Mr Stevens, in case the police try to plant evidence.'

Evans then conducted the party outside.

'Right, in the car, DC Robins, see what you can find,' instructed the DI, who started to examine the damaged nearside wing.

'Certainly looks as if the damage was a while ago, sir,' reported Carlsen after a few moments, 'there are signs of rust on the paintwork.'

'Sir, take a look at this, will you?' said Robins, 'looks like small splashes of blood here on the front passenger door and inside on the floor.'

Martin and Carlsen bent down for a closer look.

'Certainly looks like it, sir,' agreed the DI, 'I think we need our forensic boys to look at this down at the nick.'

'Mr Stevens, would you be good enough to ask Miss Glass to come outside, please?'

'Oh, what now?' the woman demanded a few moments later.

'We have found what seem to be small splashes of blood inside your car, can you explain them?'

'Olive Adams cut herself on a broken teacup after the meeting and she continued to bleed on the way home, Evans is supposed to have cleared up the mess.'

'Just to confirm, Miss Glass, do you remember what day Miss Adams cut herself and where was the cut?'

'The day of the murder, and the cut was on the back of her left hand.'

'Well, I'm afraid we're going to have to seize your car for detailed examination,' said Martin, 'we'll let you have it back as soon as possible.'

'What? You will do no such thing,' she bellowed, 'I need my car. Stevens, stop them.'

The solicitor hesitated and looked as if he wished the earth would swallow him up.

'Er, is this really necessary, chief inspector?'

'I think you already know the answer to that, Mr Stevens.'

The man looked apologetically at his client.

'You useless little man,' growled Glass at the solicitor, 'do what you like with my car, but believe me, the chief constable is going to hear about this and all of you will all be out of a job. Go on, charge me with murder now and be done with it, I dare you.'

She paused and gazed through narrowed eyes firstly at Martin and then Carlsen.

'No, I thought not,' she sneered, 'in which case, Evans, conduct these so-called gentlemen off my property once they've taken my car. I want it back tomorrow, do you understand, Mr Martin? Otherwise, I'll come down the police station and take it back myself whether you like it or not.'

Glass then stormed inside, slamming the door behind her, leaving her downcast solicitor standing in the drive with Evans.

'Oh, dear, Mr Evans, I hope we haven't spoilt your day as well,' remarked Carlsen.

'Believe me, sir, I'm used to it,' replied the butler wearily, eyes shooting skywards.

'Right, Robins, you stay here with Mr Stevens whilst I make arrangements to remove the car,' instructed Martin, 'if you wish to be present at the police station whilst we examine it, Mr Stevens, we shall be doing that as soon as I can arrange it; so if you wish to go straight there once the car is removed from here, we'll meet you.'

The man nodded.

'Meanwhile, John, we'll get back to the nick and speak to County.'

'God, what a performance,' said Martin, mopping his brow back in the office, 'on the positive side, we'll get copies of Glass's dabs off her car and with a bit of luck, they might just match those two clear prints at the murder scene. Also, we'll take a look at the pathologist's report when it arrives and see if he confirms that a cut was found on that hand.'

'Hopefully not,' said the DI, 'then Glass will have to explain where the blood came from.'

'Either way, never say die, John, if our luck does run out, well, it looks like a trip to Mr Fowler, at least for me. I thought for a moment she was going to plant one on us to be honest.'

'Silly cow, frankly I think she's a bit mental,' said Carlsen, 'one minute relatively normal, the next up like a Roman candle.'

'The world's full of barmy old ladies, John, and Malvern is no different, except that she's not that decrepit.'

'The vehicle is in the station yard, sir,' Carlsen told the DCI later at the police station, 'the distributor arm has been removed so that if the old biddy carries out her threat and comes down here, she won't be able to run off with the car. Anyway, the damage to the vehicle is not going to be critical as she admits dropping Adams off on the day anyway and there was definitely some old damage on her gatepost.'

'Yup, but it's out of our hands now, the forensic boys are coming over straight away to look at the blood stains and they're bringing a photographer with them. With a bit of luck, I'll have something positive to tell the guvnor so I can keep the chief constable off his back and mine. Stevens is downstairs waiting.'

The following morning, Carlsen answered the phone in Martin's office. It was the pathologist's clerk.

'Ah, detective inspector, no additional surprises,' said the man, 'the final report will be on its way to you in the next day or two.'

'Before you go, we were going to ask the pathologist whether he can confirm the presence of a cut on the back of Adams's left hand during his examination as was suggested by our suspect?' DI Carlsen said.

'Just a moment, I'll enquire.'

There was a brief pause and a muffled conversation at the other end of the line.

'Is it likely that our suspect is telling the truth? If so, I assume that such a minor wound would not have bled much, sir?' Carlsen queried when the pathologist came on the phone.

'Oh, I think so, if your suspect had been in that house, there would have been blood all over the place, including the car. She could never have easily cleaned it off. The victim would have bled quite a bit from the stab wounds as well. Same blood group as the victim's, so it's quite likely that your suspect is telling the truth about the source of the blood in the car.'

The DI later reported the news to Martin.

'Well, according to the pathologist, the blood in the Glass's car is definitely Olive Adams's, sir, but unfortunately for us, he thinks that if Glass had committed the murder, she would have been covered in blood as would her car.'

'I suppose not unexpected,' said Martin, 'by the way, anything interesting on the housekeeper?'

'No, Roberts has been poking around but nothing; born and bred in Malvern, married, has worked in service for most of her life, apart from looking after the kids. Her old man's a dustman, no leads there, I'm afraid. We've got a set of Black's prints and they've been taken to Worcester; they should be able to gives some news on those later today. But nothing unusual if they turn up a match at the house.'

'Haven't heard anything positive either regarding Glass's prints in the car and those found in the house,' said Martin glumly, 'and I get a horrible feeling that the news on that front will not be good. I know the place was in a terrible mess but I live in hopes.'

This was confirmed by a phone call half an hour later.

'No luck with those two clear prints on the base of the vase,' said the fingerprint officer, 'one belongs to the housekeeper and the other to the victim. No match to your suspect, I'm afraid.'

'Well, that's the lovely Leticia out of the frame, but it fits in with what we were originally told, hardly a usable fingerprint in sight in the Adams house,' commented Carlsen. The problem is where now?'

'You know, something troubles me about this case, John,' said Martin, 'not just that it rows Leticia Glass out of it, but this person, this so-called "official-looking" individual seen going into the drive of "The Camelias" in Graham Road on that day. I still wonder what that was all about? Might be worth having a chat with the local gas and electricity companies to find out whether any of their blokes were out and about in the area on the day of the murder. I imagine they would be in uniform if they were visiting a property. Roberts has already checked the nicks around the county and over the hill at Hereford to see whether it was police, but nobody admits to having paid a visit to Olive Adams on that or any other day unless it was done on the sly, too risky, and I can't imagine any copper would do that. And there's certainly no evidence that any of our blokes made a visit, authorised or otherwise. But at any rate, John, it might be worth re-visiting the witness to see if he can remember anything on top of what he told that Worcester DC. Get a detailed statement and also check any addresses that we might have missed during our local enquiries after the event; I've got to be watertight to keep Fowler at bay.'

'Right, sir, I'll take DC Weston with me, Roberts is tied up with those burglaries down in Pickersleigh. One less thing to worry about though, one of the DCs has managed to run Olive Adams's sister to ground, she's going over to identify the body at Worcester in the morning. I hope they've managed to clean it up a bit, she's in a bit of a mess. Anyhow, I'll get over there first thing.'

'Well, I'd rather you than me,' said Martin. 'Unfortunately, I'll have to pay the lovely Miss Glass a visit and tell her she's no longer under investigation, at least for now. Still, when we present her with her car all nicely cleaned up, she'll probably be much happier.'

'Oh, I do hope so, sir, cuddly as a teddy bear, I expect,' grinned Carlsen.

'Get out of here, John, or I might change my mind and send you instead.'

Chapter 10

One sunny day about a week later, a woman walked up the steps of Malvern police station and spoke to Sergeant White.

'I may have something to tell you regarding the Sweet murder,' she announced, 'could I have a word with the officer in charge please?'

'Sounds interesting, John,' said Martin, after the sergeant had arrived in the CID office and explained, 'go and have a word, will you?'

Downstairs, a blonde well-dressed woman in her thirties was sitting in the waiting room.

Detective Inspector Carlsen introduced himself.

'I understand you may have something to tell us about the Sweet murder?'

'Yes, my name is Celia Austen, I live near Thurrock's quarry and I've read in the paper that Dorothy Sweet's body has turned up there seventeen years or so after her disappearance.'

'Yes, that's right.'

'Well, I think I might have seen something on the night it all happened.'

Carlsen looked quizzical.

'Hold on a moment, please, Miss Austen, as you say many years or so have passed since Miss Sweet vanished, why has it taken so long for you to come forward?'

'I'll explain, I used to be at Malvern Girls College but now I'm an English teacher and I've been abroad teaching English to French children amongst others and mostly haven't been back home for a long time. Well, I returned to this country a few days ago, and I heard the latest news on the Sweet business when I read the Malvern Gazette. That's why you haven't heard from me before; I knew nothing about it at all when I was abroad. Nobody told me over the years, presumably because there was nothing to tell and, in any case, English newspapers are few and far between over there.'

'All right, please tell me what happened.'

'Well, I had a rented cottage just around the corner from Thurrock's quarry, still have, and I'm a bit of a bird watcher and was in the habit of frequently visiting the place to see what I could find. It's only about five minutes' walk from my little abode. On the day Miss Sweet disappeared, I was in the quarry that evening in my little bird hidey hole there for one last occasion before going abroad the next day; actually it's a large bush but with quite good visibility. Anyway, I was in there and heard voices both of which I recognised.'

'Who were they, Miss Austen?

'Miss Sweet and Miss Glass.'

'What?' Carlsen exclaimed, 'both together at the quarry?'

'Yes.'

Carlsen held up his hands.

'Will you please wait a moment? I think my chief inspector will want to hear this.'

Martin was summoned.

'Please summarise for me what you have told Mr Carlsen so far, Miss Austen,' requested the detective chief inspector.

The woman then repeated her story.

'So, what time was all this?' continued the DI.

'About nine o'clock in the evening, it was very warm and thundery with a few spots of rain, so I remember it well.'

'Where were these women in relation to you?'

'About twenty feet away, I don't think they could have seen me. I certainly couldn't see them.'

'And what were they talking about?'

'Well, in fact they were arguing.'

'About what?' said Carlsen.

'Couldn't tell, it was just the tone of their voices but I did hear the word "school" mentioned more than once.'

'And what were they doing, walking or standing still?'

'As far as I could tell, they were just standing on the footpath.'

'How long did the argument continue?'

'Oh. I suppose two or three minutes?'

'And then what happened?'

'They moved out of earshot.'

'All right, were they still arguing at that point?'

'Certainly, their voices were still raised.'

'And did anything else happen that you saw or heard as between the two women?'

'Well, a couple of minutes later, I heard Miss Sweet call out, "What are you doing?" and then I heard a cry, a sort of yelp, I suppose, and a bit of a crashing noise.'

'A crashing noise?' queried Carlsen. 'I thought you said that they had moved out of earshot.'

'Well, yes, I meant conversation wise, but the noise was quite loud like the snapping of twigs as if someone or something had fallen into a bush and the cry was quite clear.'

'You're sure it was Miss Sweet who called out?'

'Oh, yes, her voice was quite distinctive.'

'How far was your hidey hole from the quarry hut?

'Oh, I would say about ten or twelve yards, why?'

'Just background information, Miss Austen, we will need to go and have a look.

'So, after you heard the crashing noise, did you go and take a look to see what might have caused it?'

'Yes, after a few minutes, but I couldn't see anything because it was getting dark even though there were a few flashes of lightning.'

'All right, did you see or hear either of the two women again that evening.'

'No.'

'Did you see anyone else?'

'Well, as a matter of fact, I did. I saw two men by the hut there but I didn't speak to them. This was before I took up position in my hidey hole.'

'Description?'

'Didn't take much notice really, both medium height, one a bit older than the other, I think. The light wasn't too good; it was a long time ago.'

'All right, before we continue, how much did you know about this case before coming to see us, Miss Austen?' intervened Martin.

'I don't understand.'

'Well, for example, do you know the circumstances in which Miss Sweet's body was found?'

'No, I know very little about the case apart from what I read in Gazette.'

'And what did you read in the Gazette?'

'That human remains had been found at Thurrock's quarry and that they had been identified as belonging to Miss Sweet. That's it, really.'

'You see,' continued Martin, 'my point being that if this comes to court, much will be made by the defence that your memory is at fault after all this time and that you are merely making up what you think you saw or heard fit what is already known.'

'No that's not true, I know what happened.'

'All right, how well did you know these two women?'

'I was head girl at Malvern Girls College in my last year with them in 1919 so knew both women very well.'

'What was your opinion of them?'

'I liked Miss Sweet enormously, she seemed to be very efficient and would listen to any problems you might have no matter how busy she was at the time, especially if you were homesick. It was she who appointed me head girl.'

'And Miss Glass?'

'To be perfectly honest, I loathed the woman. She was spiteful and vindictive, although I grudgingly have to admit she was a good English teacher, mainly I think because the children were terrified of her. It was not unknown for her to rap a child's knuckles with a ruler and make them bleed and also beat them on the bottom with a split cane, which did the same only worse.'

'Did you fall foul of her?' Carlsen asked.

'Yes, more than once.'

'What happened?'

'Well, before I became head girl, she falsely accused me of theft on two occasions, stealing someone else's sweets in the dorm. Not a word of apology even when she discovered she was wrong and that another girl was responsible. I rather hoped something nasty would happen to her, no such luck unfortunately.'

'Were you beaten in the manner you've just described?'

'Yes, more than once, including for the missing sweets.'

'All right, apart from rumour, do you personally know how Miss Sweet and Miss Glass got on at the school?'

'Well, yes, as head girl, I was expected to make the rounds of the school to make sure that the younger girls were getting ready for bed and then report back to the duty house mistress if there was a problem. My route took me past the headmistress's study and on one occasion I heard raised voices coming from there, and to be perfectly honest I listened at the door. Miss Sweet was saying to

Miss Glass, "Stop telling me how to conduct myself and run my school, I'm the headmistress here and so long as I remain so you will kindly follow my instructions, do you understand?" There was no reply that I could make out but I heard footsteps coming towards the study door and had to make my escape. Even so, Miss Glass came storming out of the room as I walked away and demanded to know what I was doing. I told her that I was merely doing my rounds as required of me and that placated her somewhat.'

'Any other similar occasions that you remember, Miss Austen?'

'No, not specifically, but when they talked together in public, despite their best efforts they clearly didn't get on. I think Miss Glass was jealous of Miss Sweet's position, and rumour had it that Miss Glass had applied for the position of head but Miss Sweet was appointed instead.'

'Yes, so we believe, but do you know of any other persons who might be able to confirm or, otherwise, the type of behaviour you've just described?'

'Well, there's always the other teachers or, indeed, girls who were around at the time if you can find them; I find it hard to believe that someone else didn't notice what was going on.'

'All right, back to that evening at Thurrock's quarry,' continued Carlsen, 'are you absolutely sure that you saw nor heard anybody else whilst you were birdwatching apart from Miss Sweet and Miss Glass's conversation plus the two men by the hut?'

'Yes.'

'Well, thank you, Miss Austen, we will need a detailed statement which we'll take now if that's convenient. I hope you're not going off abroad again?'

'No, not anymore, Mr Carlsen, I've got an English teaching job in Malvern at the Link School. That should keep me happy for a while if I can cope with all those French and Latin enthusiasts among the teaching staff.'

'Good, because we will probably need you at court,' said the detective inspector, 'as long as you understand that your dislike of Miss Glass may tell against your evidence, to say nothing of the passage of time.'

'I understand.'

'One last question, Miss Austen, why did you not think to call the police after you heard the cry and crashing noise?'

'Well, as I said, it was almost dark and I saw nothing on my way home to suggest anything really bad had happened, despite the noise I'd heard, otherwise I would have done. I suppose I assumed that the disagreement had been resolved amicably despite the shout from Miss Sweet, and in any case I didn't have a phone at the cottage.'

After the statement had been taken and Austen had departed, both men returned to Martin's office to discuss this unexpected development.

'Well, that's a turn up for the books, sir,' remarked Carlsen.

'Yes, it certainly is, provided she's remembered it right after all this time, but it would be nice to have some corroborative evidence. I'm going to have a word with Mr Fowler on this one, we'll have to get Glass in and have a chat whether she likes it or not.'

'Best wear a suit of armour then,' commented Carlsen grimly.

'Personally, on the face of it, I think there's probably enough to charge her,' continued Martin. 'It's circumstantial but Austen puts her up at the quarry at probably about the right time or thereabouts of Sweet's murder, the body was found below where the hut is located and near where the argument took place, and Austen says that they couldn't stand each other. Glass could easily have gone to the quarry and back to the school that evening in her car, given that the doorkeeper saw her drive past his window on her return to the school. We need to establish where she went that evening. Also, the fact that Glass appears to be a bit mental and seems to hold grudges; it all adds up. Anyway, I'll speak to Fowler, he'll probably want to consult with the legal eagles. It could end up being a tricky one for a jury.'

'Nothing if not exciting police work in Malvern, eh, sir?' Carlsen remarked.

'Mm, that's one way of putting it.'

Later, Carlsen again talked to Martin.

'I didn't get a chance to discuss it before what with this Austen woman coming in but this witness regarding the Adams murder, sir, I've managed to get a detailed statement from him but there's not much more than what we already know. The description is very sketchy, still talks about an official looking male, thirties, about six feet tall, biggish, wearing a brown suit and a soft brimmed hat. That covers about two thirds of the male population of Malvern, I would imagine. He still can't explain what he means by "official", but as we know he's elderly so I don't know how much he can be relied on. I've also had a word with the local gas and electricity companies, they've no record of any of their employees being in the area so that's closed that one off.'

'Oh, well, at least we tried, John, I think we're up against a brick wall at the moment as there are no more leads. Let's hope we don't get another murder before we see the light and some clever dick comes along and suggests that we should have done this or that in the first place.

'Meanwhile, I've spoken to the guvnor regarding Sweet,' continued Martin, 'and as I thought, he agrees that there is probably enough to charge Glass, but when we've spoken to the woman the papers will go up to solicitors for a decision. So, she'll have to be bailed. To be on the safe side, I'll go to court and get a warrant then we'll nick her perhaps later today, but we'll have to go down there mob handed for she's bound to lay waste to half of Malvern when we tell her she's going to be arrested.'

A couple of hours later, warrant in hand, Martin, Carlsen and other officers arrived at Glass's address. As expected, screaming and shouting, Leticia Glass was taken struggling and handcuffed to Malvern police station where she was joined by her hapless solicitor who made fruitless efforts to placate her.

'Stevens, I demand that you arrange for my release immediately and be quick about it otherwise I will complain to your employers. As for you, Chief Inspector Martin, and you too, Inspector Carlsen, your careers are at an end, get me your chief constable on the telephone now, I wish to speak to him.'

'No, madam, I will not,' replied Martin, 'you have been lawfully arrested on a warrant issued by a magistrate and you are entitled to have a solicitor present which you have. Now, I need to ask you some questions.'

'Sadly, Miss Glass,' commented Stevens, 'I have to agree with the chief inspector, now can we get on, please?'

'All right, if you must,' Glass responded, calming a little, 'but frankly I'd prefer to live in Soviet Russia than put up with the thugs and incompetents you find in this country. And make no mistake, I shall still be writing to the chief constable, and the Home Secretary, if necessary.'

The woman was then reminded that she was under caution.

'Miss Glass, Miss Dorothy Sweet, headmistress of Malvern Girls College, disappeared on 16 June 1920, having apparently gone for an evening walk in the Malvern hills. As you also know, her remains were recently discovered in Thurrock's quarry. Can you tell me anything about that?'

'No, this is utter nonsense. I know nothing whatsoever about her death.'

'Are you sure, Miss Glass? This really is most important.'

'Of course I'm sure, I've never heard such twaddle in all my life. First you start checking typewriters then you accuse me of murdering Olive Adams or some such nonsense and now you're doing the same thing regarding Dorothy Sweet. Well, really, you ought to be in a circus the pair of you.'

The solicitor shifted uneasily in his seat and looked at his watch.

'Let's change tack for a moment, Miss Glass,' continued the chief inspector.

'How did you get on with Miss Sweet? I mean, were you on good terms?'

'Naturally.'

'All the time?'

'We had minor disagreements, what of it?'

'Well, information we have in our possession, Miss Glass, suggests that your relationship with Miss Sweet was strained to say the least. Is that true?'

'Who told you that?'

'Our sources don't matter, please answer the question.'

'As I said, we had our disagreements.'

'But these disagreements often ended in shouting matches didn't they, Miss Glass?'

'All right, sometimes, but it was never my fault.'

'Oh, so Miss Sweet was entirely responsible, was she?'

'She thought she knew everything, sometimes she had to be told.'

'It wasn't just Miss Sweet you argued with, was it?' Martin continued, 'you have a reputation of being bad tempered and one who holds a grudge against people who dare to defy you. That's true, isn't it ?'

'Stuff and nonsense, it's a pack of lies. I repeat, who have you been talking to?'

Ignoring the question, he continued.

'While we're about it, did you ever send a threatening letter to Miss Sweet just before her death? THIS letter, please examine it,' said Martin, pushing the typewritten sheet and envelopes across the table, together with a copy for the solicitor.

Leticia Glass paused.

'No,' she replied in a low voice.

'Really? Are you certain?'

There was silence and Glass looked hard at her solicitor.

'Miss Glass?'

'Yes, all right, I did send it.'

'Why?'

'Because, well, because I thought she was defrauding the school.'

95

The detectives looked incredulous.

'Defrauding the school, why on earth should you think that?' the DCI asked.

'In the safe in the headmistress's study, we kept a good deal of petty cash for everyday expenses at the school to save always going to the bank. One day, I was looking at the cash book and I thought I found some discrepancies, money missing, that kind of thing. Well, since Miss Sweet and I, apart from Colonel Phillips, who was then chairman of the governors, were the only ones who had access to the safe, and as it wasn't me I assumed it must be her than rather than the colonel.'

'Why didn't you confront her or simply ask her whether she had noticed a problem with the cash book?'

'Because I wanted to frighten her. '

'But why? After all, she would have realised the letter was likely to be from you rather than Colonel Phillips surely.'

'May be, but I just wanted to keep her guessing for a while. In fact, I was planning to talk to her about it the evening she disappeared. The stupid truth is, I made an error because I rechecked the cash book against the monies that evening after I returned to the school and found I had made a silly mistake; everything was as it should be, so of course I should never have sent the letter.'

'But the letter was sent and that could be considered to be verging on blackmail, Miss Glass, even though she may never have received it. So, what was the meaning of: "you know what you have to do" on this sheet of paper?'

'I hoped she might resign and leave the headship open to me. In the event, it would have had to be me who resigned and that would have been the end of my career.'

'Did Miss Sweet show any sign of having received any letter?'

'No, she did not.'

'Which typewriter did you use?'

'One at the school out of the stationery cupboard; it eventually went to one of the other teachers, I'm not sure who.'

'Yes, we now have it, it has a fault which distinguishes it from other machines and that appears on the letter. The typewriter was eventually passed to a Miss Stubbs, one of your former colleagues.

'To continue, the letter was just one part of a vendetta you were conducting against Miss Sweet at Malvern Girls' College, that's true, isn't it?'

'No.'

'Are you certain about that, Miss Glass?'

The woman stared into space for a moment.

'Look I've agreed that I sent the letter without properly checking the facts but I was not conducting a vendetta against her, chief inspector. To suggest otherwise is ridiculous.'

'Well, it ended up being sent to Miss Sweet's parents, which upset them. How did that happen?'

'I'm sorry that they saw it, obviously it was not my intention. But it's the school secretary's writing on the outer envelope, after Dorothy's disappearance she must have sent it on without reading it.'

'All right, returning to the evening of Miss Sweet's disappearance, did you to go for a walk up at Thurrock's quarry, perhaps after leaving your car up there? After all, you were seen returning to the college by the doorkeeper in your vehicle later that evening.'

'No, I suppose this is another of your fanciful ideas. Yes, I did go out in my car, I can't remember where now but it certainly was not the quarry.'

'Not fanciful, Miss Glass, our information is that you in fact went to the quarry that evening and met with Miss Sweet?'

'I told you I did not go there, let alone meet anyone. Who says I did?'

'It doesn't matter who, Miss Glass, you were heard arguing with Miss Sweet on the footpath near the hut, and the same evening Miss Sweet disappeared and was not seen again.'

'How dare you accuse me of being responsible for Dorothy Sweet's death?' You stupid man, how dare you? I didn't walk or meet anybody up at the quarry that evening and I will not tolerate this nonsense any longer, I'm going home.'

Leticia Glass pushed her chair back and attempted to leave.

'You're not going anywhere, Miss Glass, until I've finished with you, now sit down,' ordered Martin firmly.

Ignoring him, she almost pushed her solicitor off his chair as she attempted to walk out of the room.

'Stop her, DC Taylor, please.'

The detective who had been sitting in on the interview got up and grabbing her by the arm and forced her back to her chair.

'Help,' she screamed, 'help.'

There was a pounding of feet along the cell passage, followed by a loud banging on the door of the room.

'Everything all right, sir?' a voice called anxiously.

'Yes, everything is all right, everything is under control,' he called, as the woman once more tried to leave her chair with Taylor, the solicitor and Carlsen attempting to restrain her.

'I would suggest, chief inspector, that my client is too upset to answer any further questions and that, in any event, she is not required to do so,' Stevens said after his client had finally returned to her seat.

'Fifteen minutes, Mr Stevens, we will then resume.'

'Well,' commented Carlsen over a strong cup of tea, 'follow that.'

'She's all bluster when she's in a tight corner, John. Anyhow, I think we'll bail her, we're not going to get anything further out of her the state she's in. We'll have to see what legal advice we get and get her back here in a couple of weeks, hopefully to stick her on the sheet.'

'Believe you me, Mr Martin,' said Glass icily when told that she was being released. 'I shall take you all to court for assault and that's just the beginning. If I have to write to the Prime Minister then I shall do so. But one way or another, I shall get justice and you will both go to prison for your crimes, do you understand? Well, DO YOU? she shouted.

'She's completely barmy, sir,' said Carlsen after the woman had left, 'there's no doubt in my mind that she fell out with Dorothy Sweet and decided that she had to go on the tenuous grounds that she didn't run the school according to Glass's ideas. She just lost her temper up at the quarry that evening and that was that. She also couldn't add up when it came to the accounts. All in all, a nasty bit of work.'

'Incidentally, not remembering where she'd been with the car has scuppered any chance of a credible alibi; I don't think we'll tell her that though.'

'Yes, I noticed that,' replied the DCI, 'but killing Sweet didn't do the delightful Leticia much good, she still didn't get the headship, and presumably that's why after a few years, she retired relatively young.'

'With a bit of luck, sir, I hope that will soon be a permanent state of affairs with the help of the hangman.'

Three weeks later, after legal advice, Leticia Glass was charged with the murder of Dorothy Sweet.

'She'll fight it all the way, sir,' remarked Carlsen later, 'no question about that.'

'Yes, but I think we can make it stick provided Celia Austen does her bit,' replied Martin, 'it's got to go before a jury it really has. Trouble is that the defence will make much of Austen's feelings about the woman and how long it's been, but there we are. You never can tell with juries, depends how persuasive the defence brief is.'

Chapter 11

One day in March 1938, Detective Chief Inspector Martin and Detective Inspector Carlsen walked up the steps to Worcester Assizes for the trial of Leticia Glass.

'Looks like our brief is going to be old Jameson,' remarked Martin after examining the court list, 'he's been a KC for a number of years, and is a good one, takes trouble to get things right, I've had dealings with him before.'

'Who's the opposition?' asked Carlsen.

'Symes, who can be a bit nasty at times, doesn't like coppers, I think even the judges are a bit frightened of him. I reckon he's a bit too fond of the jungle juice and takes it out on everyone else the morning after, including me in the past. He's just been made a KC, so that'll probably make him worse. We'll have to see whether this Judge Clifton bloke can cope with him.'

'Good morning, gentlemen, Laurence Jameson, I think we've met before,' said a voice a moment or two later.

'Good morning, sir, indeed we have, how are you?' replied Martin to a tall, slim man wearing a wig who had approached them.

'Oh, still scratching a living, thank you. It's a not guilty, chief inspector, could be tricky this one, you haven't given me much to go on but I bear you no malice. The defence will make much of the passage of time, plus the fact that our star witness disliked the defendant, to put it mildly; is Miss Austen here yet?'

'Just walking through the door now, sir,' said Carlsen.

'All right, I will also be calling Miss Smith, she can give evidence of this woman's character. That probably won't be until tomorrow though, but if you just ensure she's available please if she's not already here.

'And I shall want you to give evidence of arrest, Mr Martin, once the opening speeches are done with, and Mr Carlsen you may be required but we'll have to see. I will need to take you through the interview with the defendant, chief inspector, to show her history with the dead woman, possibly you too, inspector. I may not require Miss Austen until the morning, but again she'll need to wait

100

just in case. Apart from the pathologist, the other witnesses, your doctor etc. can be released; the defence is not challenging their evidence. See you in court.'

After a moment's chat with Celia Austen, Jameson was gone.

Following the court usher confirming a not guilty plea, Martin and Carlsen settled down to wait. A nervous Celia Austen sat some way away, alternately glancing at her watch and the court room door. Stephanie Smith also sat some distance away. Later that afternoon after the completion of opening speeches, Martin was called to give evidence of arrest. When he had finished, Michael Symes, defence counsel, stood up, leant forward and eyed the chief inspector.

'Ah, Mr Martin,' he began, 'how conversant are you with judges' rules on the interviewing of suspects?'

'Extremely conversant, Your Honour.'

'In that case, officer, did you caution the defendant before the interview commenced?' Symes continued.

'Yes, Your Honour.'

'Repeat the caution, please.'

The detective did so.

'Which, as you have just quoted, includes the words "you are not obliged to say anything unless you wish to do so", yes?'

'Yes, Your Honour.'

'In that case, why did you exert unfair pressure on my client to confess to a crime that she didn't commit in order to "clear the books", as I think the police saying goes, especially after so much time has passed?'

'Your Honour, I did not exert any unfair pressure on Miss Glass, her solicitor was present throughout and nothing unlawful occurred.

'But you upset my client so much that she broke down and the interview had to be terminated by Mr Stevens. Is that not so, chief inspector?' Symes continued.

'Yes, Your Honour, Miss Glass did indeed become very upset, but the interview then immediately ceased at the request of Mr Stevens and was not resumed that day on my decision.'

'But had you not bullied her the question of my client becoming hysterical in the first place would not have arisen, would it?'

'Miss Glass was not bullied, Your Honour, I treated her perfectly reasonably,' replied the DCI.

'But the interview ended with you or your officers assaulting the defendant despite the best efforts of her solicitor. That's true, isn't it?'

'No, Your Honour, we used the minimum amount of force to restrain her.'

'No further questions, Your Honour,' said Symes who sighed and sat down.

'Re-examination, Mr Jameson?' Judge Clifton enquired.

The prosecuting barrister rose to his feet, adjusting his wig and half glasses.

'Mr Martin, you've just said that you had to restrain Miss Glass, what action or actions prompted this?'

'Well, Miss Glass became very agitated and tried to leave the interview room before we had finished and had to be restrained by my officers.'

'And then what happened?'

'Once Miss Glass had been returned to her seat, Mr Stevens, the defendant's solicitor, intervened and asked me to stop the questioning, which I did. And even though I had originally intended to restart the interview after a fifteen-minute break, I decided not to proceed due to Miss Glass's state of mind. So, as I have already said, the interview was discontinued. Miss Glass was then bailed pending legal advice.'

'Indeed, thank you, officer, no further questions, Your Honour.'

'I would now like to call the Home Office pathologist, Your Honour,' continued Jameson.

Mr Justice Clifton glanced at his pocket watch which he produced from under a pile of papers.

'Yes, but not today, Mr Jameson, court is adjourned to ten o'clock tomorrow. The defendant's bail conditions remain the same.'

Leticia Glass remained seated, staring into space and had to be urged to move by the dock officer.

'Phew,' said Martin outside the court.

'Bit of a grilling, sir?' commented Carlsen.

'Yes, Symes was up to his old tricks, suggested we were brutes etc. etc. the usual rubbish. But the fact that her solicitor was present during the interview didn't help the defence case. Tomorrow, it'll be Austen's and Smith's turn, I hope they're both up to it, especially Austen, but it doesn't look as if you'll be needed, John.'

This was confirmed a little later by Jameson.

'Presumably, the defence doesn't think I can add anything,' commented the DI drily, 'looks like Symes has given up on the brutality angle.'

The following morning, an anxious Celia Austen arrived early and approached the chief inspector in the court precincts.

'I'm sorry, Mr Martin, but I can't go through with this you know, I just can't.'

'But why?'

'I'm frightened it's all going to go wrong.'

Martin tried to reassure.

'I understand why you're nervous, Miss Austen, but you will be guided through your evidence by our counsel, and the judge will make sure that you are not expected to answer any unreasonable questions put to you by the defence.'

'What happens if I refuse to give evidence?'

'The judge could find you in contempt of court and imprison you. After all, this is not a minor matter but a murder trial. We did make it clear when you came to us that you would be expected to give evidence.'

'Well, I suppose I'll have to go through with it,' she replied reluctantly. 'Oh, dear, this is awful.'

'Thank you and good luck,' said Martin gently.

'Oh, dear, Austen IS getting cold feet, we'd better warn Jameson,' continued the chief inspector, 'I'll try and talk to him after he has finished with the pathologist.'

Later, after reassurance from the prosecuting barrister, Celia Austen entered the witness box and nervously gave her evidence.

When she had finished, Mr Symes rose to his feet, stuck his thumbs in his waistcoat and stared at the witness for several seconds.

'Miss Austen,' he began, 'you said in your evidence that you disliked Miss Glass during you time at Malvern Girls' College, in fact you used the word "loathed". Were you still carrying this feeling of loathing, as you put it, when you left the college?'

'Yes.'

'Why?'

'Because, well, because she was one of those truly horrid people you never really forget.'

Leticia Glass looked annoyed and opened her mouth as if to say something but changed her mind.

'Quite so,' continued Symes 'and you also said quite the opposite in that you would have done almost anything for the late Miss Sweet because she was so nice. Is that right?'

'Yes.'

'Including indirectly lying for her?'

'No,' Austen answered quickly.

'Oh, come, come, Miss Austen, do you really expect the court to believe that you are prepared to be even handed in the matter of Miss Sweet's murder when it comes to identifying her killer?'

'Yes.'

'So, you are quite prepared, are you not, to see the defendant hang in order to satisfy your craving for revenge?'

'No, no, I'm not,' replied Austen, putting her hands up to her face and beginning to shake.

'The truth is, you had, maybe still have, one of these silly schoolgirl crushes on the late Miss Sweet and are prepared, even after all this time, to tell preposterous lies on her behalf. That's true, isn't it?'

'No.'

'Were you beaten at school by Miss Glass?'

'Yes.'

'Frequently?'

'Quite often, yes.'

'Another motive, I suggest, for lying about the defendant.'

'No.'

'All right, let us move on to the evening of Miss Sweet's disappearance in that you say you were in your bird watching hidey hole and could hear voices on the path nearby.'

'Yes.'

'Bird watching in the middle of a thunderstorm?' asked Symes incredulously.

'Yes, but it wasn't thundering that much, although there was a lot of lightning and a bit of rain.'

'All three go together, do they not, Miss Austen?'

'Objection, Your Honour,' intervened Jameson, 'the witness's knowledge of the weather is not on trial here.'

'Yes, stick to matters with which the witness may be able to assist us, Mr Symes,' agreed the judge.

Symes bowed slightly and smirked.

'Miss Austen,' he continued, 'what do you know about redstarts?'

Celia Austen looked startled.

'Well, they're a kind of bird, you sometimes see them up at the quarry. They have red tails.'

'And peregrines?'

'They are raptors and occasionally visit the quarry and sometimes nest there but they are quite rare now.'

'Mr Symes, this is not a nature ramble,' intervened the judge sourly, 'get to the point.'

'Your Honour, I am merely trying to establish the credentials of the witness as a bird watcher. It appears that she is, as indeed am I.'

'Very well, continue.'

'I'm grateful, Your Honour.'

'Bird watcher or not, Miss Austen,' continued the defence counsel, 'do you honestly expect the court to believe that in the middle of a noisy storm, you were able to identify the voices of two people that presumably you had not heard for over a year?'

'Yes.'

'You said in your evidence that the two women were arguing, why do you say that?'

'Because they were talking very loudly.'

'So, what were they arguing about?'

'I don't know.'

'But if their voices were raised and they were arguing why could you not hear what they were saying?'

'I don't know.'

'Well, I suggest to you, Miss Austen, that the reason you couldn't hear what was going on is because you've made the whole thing up in the first place and can't remember what nonsense you intended to tell this court in the witness box. In short, Miss Austen, you are a vengeful fantasist and an unmitigated liar, are you not?'

'No, no, I'm not,' she replied feebly, looking pale and continuing to shake.

'Yes, she is,' shouted Leticia Glass from the dock.

There was a sharp intake of breath from the packed public gallery.

'That's enough, the defendant will remain silent,' interjected the judge, 'I will not tolerate interruptions in my court, otherwise I will have you taken down to the cells. Do you understand?'

'Yes,' Glass growled.

'You will get your chance to speak later in the trial should you wish it,' he added.

'Continue, Mr Symes.'

'Thank you, Your Honour, but no further questions.'

'Call Stephanie Smith,' intoned Jameson.

'Miss Smith,' commenced the crown prosecutor once the woman had settled in the witness box and taken the oath. 'Thank you for attending court, I would like you to answer some questions regarding the defendant's character based on your own knowledge of Miss Glass.'

'Firstly, how long have you known the defendant?'

'Oh, since the 1890s when we were at school together.'

'And where was that?'

'At Cherrywood near Hereford.'

'And has that relationship continued until now?'

'Only intermittently.'

'And why is that?'

'Well, because we're not friends and have only met once or twice away from professional duties.'

'You say that you are not friends, again why?'

'Because we don't get on.'

'Explain, please.'

'Well, over the years, there have been one or two incidents that have rather soured our relationship.'

'What incidents, Miss Smith?'

'Well, firstly, there was an occasion at Cherrywood school which involved a child being pushed down the stairs.'

'Who did that involve?'

'Several children.

'Including you?'

'Yes.'

'And also Miss Glass?'

'As it turned out, no.'

'But how was the matter resolved?'

'Leticia left the school.

'Why, do you know?'

'She was blamed for the incident.'

'Why, Miss Smith?'

'Because she had a bad reputation and some children lied to get her into trouble.'

'Including you.'

'To my eternal regret, yes.'

'All right, let us move beyond the years at Cherrywood.'

'When did you next meet the defendant?'

'At the Abbey School in Malvern some years later.'

'On what occasion was that?'

'The headmistress wanted to set up a liaison group with surrounding schools and Leticia was involved in that, as was I, being headmistress at Bushley school.'

'And what happened?'

'There was a row between the two of us, largely, I'm afraid, because of something I rather foolishly said.'

'And what was that?'

'I mentioned the Cherrywood incident in front of our guests at the first meeting.'

'And what was Miss Glass's reaction?'

'She was furious, saying words to the effect that I should never have brought the subject up, which of course, I shouldn't, at least not at that point.'

'What happened next?'

'Well, we parted after the meeting and I didn't expect to see her again until the next gathering.'

'But you did see her, where and when was that?'

'The following Sunday, she suddenly turned up at my school unannounced.'

'And what happened?'

'She demanded to know where she could find some of the girls who were involved in the Cherrywood incident.'

'And did you tell her?'

'Two of them were dead, including Fiona Clerk, the one who was pushed down the stairs and I denied that I knew where the other one, Olive Adams, lived.

'How would you describe Miss Glass's behaviour the day she visited you?

'Bad tempered.'

'Can you tell the court what happened a few days later?'

'Yes, I received an unpleasant letter from Leticia.'

'Relating to what?'

'The encounter we had at Bushley.'

'This letter,' said Jameson, waving it in the air towards the jury, 'exhibit one in your bundle, Your Honour.'

'Yes, thank you Mr Jameson, I think I can count to one,' responded the judge drily.

'Members of the jury, you too have a copy.'

'If the court will permit, Your Honour, Miss Smith, will you read out the contents from your copy of the letter please?'

The judge nodded, and the witness did so.

'And what was your reaction to the letter?'

'I was rather frightened.'

'And what did you think she might do next?'

Symes jumped to his feet.

'Objection, Your Honour, my learned friend is asking the witness for an opinion as to my client's future behaviour.'

'Sustained, come along, Mr Jameson, you know better than that. Kindly rephrase the question or move on.'

'Apologies, Your Honour.'

'He knows exactly what he's doing,' whispered Carlsen in Martin's ear as they sat in the public gallery, 'trying to impress the jury as to her bad character; let's hope they go along with it.'

'Yes, crafty old devil.'

'And was that the last time you had contact with the defendant?' continued Jameson.

'Yes, apart from professionally.'

'And what are your feelings now about Leticia Glass?'

'I think she's mean spirited; in fact I rather pity her.'

'I don't want your pity, Stephanie,' screamed Leticia Glass, bringing both fists crashing down on the front of the dock, 'you were a stupid woman then and you are still.'

'The defendant will be quiet,' roared the judge, 'this is your final warning. I will not tolerate any more interruptions in this court. If it happens again, I will commit you to prison for contempt, do you understand?'

'Yes,' hissed Miss Glass, still glaring at the witness.

'Thank you, Miss Smith. Please stay there, my learned friend may wish to ask you some questions.'

'Mr Symes?' said the judge.

'Just a few questions, Your Honour.'

'Miss Smith, having received the letter from the defendant, did you contact the police?'

'No.'

'And why was that?'

'I don't really know; I just didn't consider it necessary at the time.'

'Well, I suggest that the reason that you didn't contact the police is because you weren't really frightened at all.'

'No, that's not true.'

'So, have you received any further letters threatening or otherwise from the defendant over the years?'

'No.'

'Have you ever been assaulted or threatened with assault by the defendant?'

'No, I have not.'

'And, finally, why should the court believe your story about your relationship and associated matters with the defendant when you admit you lied at Cherrywood and were in part at least responsible for her expulsion?'

'Because I was a child then and children grow up. As I say, I deeply regret what happened.'

'No further questions, Your Honour.'

'That is the case for the Crown, Your Honour,' said Jameson, 'unless my learned friend has any objections, may Miss Austen and Miss Smith be released, please?'

'Yes, they may. Will the defendant be giving evidence, Mr Symes?' enquired the judge.

'No, Your Honour, she will not.'

'Will you be calling any other witnesses for the defence?'

'No, Your Honour.'

'In that case, final submissions at ten o'clock tomorrow morning, please. Court is adjourned.'

'Well done, Miss Austen, all over now,' commented Carlsen outside the court.

'And you too, Miss Smith,' as the former headmistress disappeared out of the door.

Austen nodded and was also gone, but there were still tears in her eyes.

'Well, Symes put her through the grinder, all right, sir' commented Carlsen. 'On the other hand, these barristers have to be careful, if they overdo it with the witness, the jury make take the opposite tack and convict out of sympathy. Still, Stephanie Smith did all right. I think everyone recognised that she is a thoroughly decent woman.'

'Morning, gentlemen,' said Mr Jameson in the court precincts at about a quarter to ten the following day, 'any sign of our defendant? Your colleagues downstairs have not seen her yet and she hasn't spoken to Mr Symes.'

'I'll check, sir,' replied Martin looking at his watch.

'John, ring the nick and get Roberts or someone to go around to her address, maybe she's ill or something.'

That morning, Glass's butler, Evans, walked as usual to the shops in Church Street to buy a few items and the Gazette, the latter anticipating in banner headlines the impending end of the trial. Although the proceedings were never mentioned by his employer, he could feel the tension and wondered what would become of him if the worst happened. Having completed his tasks, he ambled slowly back along Como Road only to find a police car parked in the drive of the house with DS Roberts awaiting him.

'What's happened, Mr Roberts?' he asked.

'Where's Miss Glass this morning? Have you seen her? She's not turned up at court.'

'I'm sure she must have gone, sir, her car's not here. It was sitting in the drive as I went to the shops and she was still in the house. She normally leaves about a quarter to nine to allow plenty of time to get to Worcester.'

'I can hear the sound of a car engine, where's that coming from? Wait a minute,' Roberts said, looking around anxiously, 'where's the garage, Mr Evans?'

'Around the back, sir, on the left,' replied the man pointing.

Roberts hurried to the rear of the house and immediately noticed wisps of pale blue smoke drifting into the morning air from under the garage door with an engine clearly audible in the background.

'Help me get it open, quick,' instructed the detective.

But the double doors wouldn't budge.

'It's probably locked from the inside, is there a spare key?'

'I'll get it, Mr Roberts.'

'Hurry, Mr Evans,' urged the sergeant who put his shoulder to the heavy doors, but again without success.

The butler soon returned and Roberts, after some difficulty, managed to get them open, the key on the inside of the lock jangling as it hit the garage floor.

Smoke almost obscured the car, and in the front seat sat Leticia Glass slumped over the steering wheel.

'Get an ambulance as quick as you can,' ordered Roberts, opening the driver's door and trying to drag Glass from the seat, meanwhile switching off the car engine. Roberts felt for a pulse but there was none. Leaving the woman where she was and coughing and spluttering with handkerchief to mouth, Roberts backed out of the garage, and a few moments later the distant sound of the bell of an approaching ambulance could be heard. The vehicle soon appeared and crunched to a halt in front of the house. Two ambulance men went into the garage, but after a moments perusal of the body, confirmed that she was beyond saving.

'Oh, Christ, what a bloody mess,' said Sergeant Roberts, who was still struggling to get his breath.

Meanwhile, Evans stood in the drive, covering his face with a large handkerchief.

'Oh, madam, madam, what have you done?' he repeated over and over again.

'Go and sit down inside, Mr Evans, it won't do any good you staying out here,' suggested the sergeant, gently putting an arm around the butler's shoulder, 'I'll have someone sit with you as soon as I can. Meanwhile, I need to use your phone, please.'

The man nodded and shuffled miserably inside.

A few moments later and with some difficulty, Roberts spoke to DCI Martin.

'Sir, bad news, Glass is dead, gassed herself in her car, I called an ambulance but it was too late.'

There was a long pause followed by a sigh at the other end of the line.

'Oh, no. All right, sarge, set the ball rolling with the doctor etc. DI Carlsen will be over straight away, I've got to sort things out this end before I get there myself.'

Martin then imparted the bad news to Jameson.

'All right, Mr Martin, I'll inform Mr Symes and the judge. Wait here, please, His Honour may want to speak to you.'

Five minutes later, Martin was ordered into court, the jury having been dismissed and the court cleared. The judge motioned him to the witness box.

'This is informal, chief inspector, you're not under oath, just tell me what has happened.'

Martin explained.

'Ah, well, this is sad and most unfortunate, our thoughts are with the defendant's family if she has any, Mr Martin. Obviously, we've now got to wait for you and the coroner to do your work and for a report to be submitted to the court. Meanwhile, this trial is adjourned sine die.'

'What now, Mr Martin?' enquired Diana Davies who had been waiting outside court.

'Not at the moment, Miss Davies, please, there will be a press conference in Malvern later.'

Another three quarters of an hour passed before Carlsen appeared in the driveway of Glass's house, where two constables were standing guard. He spoke to both.

'Now, it won't be long before the press sniff out that something is going on, so no one comes in without my authority unless they're police, understand? DCI Martin will be along shortly. But let in Doc. Rogers when he arrives.'

Roberts was standing by the front door awaiting instructions.

'Has she been examined by the police doctor yet?' the DI asked as both men went around to the garage.

'He's on his way, sir, I've left her where she is at the moment until you and he have had a look. Photographers are also on their way and I've told the coroner's officer. Oh, I can't find a note at the moment but I suppose there might be one in the car.'

'All right, good.'

Doctor Rogers soon appeared.

'Nothing out of the ordinary, Mr Carlsen, carbon monoxide, of course,' he said after spending some time in the garage. 'Naturally, there will have to be a post-mortem; she was standing trial for murder, wasn't she?' Yes, well, it'll save the hangman a job, I suppose. I'll get the paperwork to you as soon as I can. Death certified at 11:20 a.m.'

'Cynical old bastard, he really is,' Carlsen muttered under his breath as the doctor departed, Gladstone bag in hand, 'he was just as bad at the Adams murder.'

'Well, he's got a point, sir,' said Roberts.

'Maybe, but he always gets his timing wrong. So, when the undertakers get here, we'll shift the body out of it once the DCI, the photographers and coroner's officer have had a look. I'll have to fend off the press until the guvnor speaks to them. He'll be here as soon as he escapes from court.'

Meanwhile, Evans sat pale and shaking in the kitchen accompanied by a constable.

'No blame can be laid at your door, Mr Evans, you couldn't possibly have anticipated this,' said the detective inspector, 'have you got anywhere you can go and stay?'

'There's my brother, sir, he lives over at Hereford, I can probably go to him. Oh, this is terrible, sir.'

'Did Miss Glass give any clue that she might attempt suicide?' asked Carslen quietly.

'Nothing, sir, nothing at all. She was obviously worried by the trial, it was written all over her, but she never talked about it.'

'Now is not the time, but we'll eventually want a statement from you, Mr Evans, just for the coroner, you understand. If you just leave us the address of your brother.'

The old man nodded.

'Did Miss Glass have any relatives that you know of?'

'No, I don't think so, apart from her brother, who she didn't get on with. He lives just around the corner, I'll give you his address; anyway, she certainly didn't talk of anyone else and none came here.'

At that moment, DCI Martin appeared at the door.

'What needs doing, John?'

'It's all in hand, sir, but I thought you might want to have a look at Glass before we move the body. No note found so far. We need to tell her brother, who apparently lives nearby, useful for identifying the body; I'll get Sergeant Roberts on to it.'

Martin then went around to the garage.

'Poor old cow,' he remarked, emerging from the garage after a couple of minutes. 'All right, once the photo boys have finished, we'll get the car out of the garage and give it a good search, there might just be a note. If not, we'll have to look in the house.'

Fifteen minutes later, photographs having been taken, the coroner's officer having attended and the body removed, Roberts reversed the car out of the garage and he and Carlsen searched it.

'Still no note found, sir,' reported Carlsen, after a few minutes. 'Suggests that she decided to kill herself on the spur of the moment.'

'Yes, well, we can arrange for the car to be taken down the nick for a proper search just in case we've missed something.'

At that moment, one of the constables came around the corner and spoke to Martin.

'Sir, there's a Mr Stevens outside, says he's Miss Glass's solicitor and there is a bit of a crowd building up, mostly journalists, I think.'

'Right, John, you deal with Stevens and I'll come around and talk to the press.'

'All right, ladies and gentlemen,' Martin said to the noisy crowd at the front of the house. I have nothing to tell you at the moment other than there's been a fatality. I will be holding a press conference at the police station at 2:00 p.m.'

A babble of questions broke out, which Martin ignored.

'This is a bit of a shock, inspector,' commented the solicitor, 'Mr Symes rang me up and gave me the news; I couldn't believe it.'

'Frankly, neither can we, sir, there's no indication as to precisely why, although presumably she thought things were not going her way.'

'Yes, I think that's quite possible. We were probably within a day of the jury being sent out and I expect that alarmed her. She was not a pleasant woman but I wouldn't have wanted things to end like this.'

'These people are all still waiting around,' said Carlsen a few moments later, 'I think we need a some more PCs up here just in case. Roberts, get on to the nick, give my compliments to Sergeant Green and ask him sort something out. I suppose it won't be long before Fowler gets on the blower and starts grinding his teeth, so we'll get back to the nick as soon as possible and I'll get ready for the press conference. You know it's amazing how upset old Evans is, considering that she treated him like dirt a lot of the time; funny thing human nature.'

Back at the police station, just as Martin was preparing for the press conference, the phone rang. As anticipated, it was the detective superintendent and Martin groaned inwardly.

'I hear on the grapevine that this woman Glass has done away with herself, do we know why?' Fowler asked, wasting no time on preliminaries.

'No obvious reason, sir, except maybe she was worried about the outcome of the trial. She failed to turn up at court and when we went around to check her out, she was dead in her car, no note anywhere.'

'This is no good at all, Mr Martin, won't be long before the press start blaming us for harassment or some such nonsense, you know what these buggers are like. So, are we watertight?'

'Should be, our witness Austen gave her evidence yesterday and closing speeches would probably have finished today; that would have only left the judge's summing up. Anyhow, I'm holding a press conference this afternoon, 2.00pm, I'll let you know how it goes, sir.'

'Yes, keep me posted, so I can tell my guvnor what's going on.'

Shortly before 2.00 p.m., detectives Martin and Carlsen opened the press conference to the usual cacophony of shouted questions.

'Why did she kill herself, chief inspector? Don't you think it might have been because she was innocent? Were you harassing her?'

Martin held up his hands.

'As you know, she was standing trial for murder, but it's not for me to prejudge what the court's verdict might have been and, no, I don't consider police were harassing her, we carried out a murder investigation just as we would in any other similar criminal case.'

After further questions, the group of journalists, having failed to extract any further information, finally thinned out and departed.

'Hopefully, that'll keep 'em at bay for a little while, John, while but sooner or later, they'll be back asking more damn silly questions, especially that bloke from Berrows; my ears are still ringing.'

'Well, apart from the usual paperwork and reports to the coroner and the court, sir, I reckon that's about it on the Sweet murder, nothing much else we can do.'

'Yeah, let's hope that Mr Fowler agrees and we can get on with something else like the Adams case and we're no further forward with that one at the moment.

'I have to admit though that justice hasn't been done, John, it would have been interesting to know what verdict the jury would have brought in. Now it's all left up in the air.'

Chapter 12

Enid Perks tossed and turned and stared at the empty space in the bed where her husband should have been.

It was past 1.00 a.m. and John Perks should have been home long ago. He was on early shift at Worcester engine shed the following morning and the Great Western Railway didn't take kindly to latecomers. He had said he was going to the pub for a drink with his mates as he often had before but somehow she didn't believe him. And he had never been this late previously and she was worried. After very little sleep and after six o'clock had come and gone without any sign of him, she went to Worcester police station.

'A missing person over at the smoke which might be of interest, sir,' said Sergeant White to the late turn inspector at Malvern that afternoon, 'seems he came over to these parts occasionally. A bloke called John Perks, reported missing this morning.'

'All right, sarge, give me the details and I'll pass it on to the troops.'

Later, a man walked up the steps of the police station and spoke to the sergeant on the desk.

'I thought I'd better hand this in,' he announced, waving a brown wallet.

'Oh, yes, where did you find that?'

'Well, I work in the Priory garden, like, and there it was by one of the gravestones. Got no name in it but there's a photo.'

'OK, I'll take your details and if has not been claimed after a month, you can have it, if you want it. Unless it turns out to be stolen, of course.'

'No, I don't think I'll bother, thanks.'

After the man had gone, Sergeant White glanced at the photo of a middle-aged man but it rang no bells.

'Oh, what have you got there, sarge?' DCI Martin asked casually, having just walked in.

'Just a wallet that was handed in a short while ago, sir, got a photo of a bloke in it but I've no idea who he is. No name, no cash, but I'm about to check lost property.'

'Let's have a look,' said the DCI.'

Martin shook his head.

'No, means nothing to me, let me take it upstairs and I'll show it around the office, maybe somebody will recognise him.'

'Right, any offers on the photograph in this wallet?' enquired Martin in the CID office.

After a brief glance, people shook their heads.

'Oh, I know him, sir,' said Roberts who had just arrived, 'he owns that quarry where Sweet was found.'

'Name?'

'Thurrock, Jesse Thurrock, middle aged bloke, lives in that big place in Grange Road, Mr Carlsen and I called there on the way back from the quarry on the day the body was discovered.'

'Oh, yes, I remember,' said Martin, handing the wallet over, 'anyway, take it back to Sergeant White downstairs, he can send a PC around to Thurrock and ask him about it.'

Chapter 13

Late the following morning, the phone rang in the DCI's office.

'Oh, is that the chief detective in the case of Olive Adams?' a female voice at the other end of the phone enquired.

Martin acknowledged that it was.

'I hope you don't mind my ringing you but I'm Olive's sister, Ethel Adams. I met your Inspector Carlsen at Worcester when I had to identify Olive's body.'

'Oh, yes, of course, I'm Detective Chief Inspector Martin, what can I do for you?'

'Have you solved the case yet by any chance?'

'No, madam, I'm afraid we haven't yet but we're ever hopeful.'

'Well, I've found something and I wonder whether we could discuss it up at Olive's house?'

'Oh, I'll come up now if that's convenient?'

'Yes, please do.'

Five minutes later, Martin arrived at "The Camelias".

'The house is still a bit of a mess, I'm afraid, chief inspector, I want to sell it but there's all these blood stains everywhere. Who's going to want to buy this house of horrors? Frankly, it terrifies me just coming in here.'

'Yes, I understand that but you could get the place professionally cleaned, walls re-papered and so on, that might help. Believe it or not, some people want to buy such places simply because of what has occurred in them.'

'Oh, how grizzly, yes, I suppose I could get some cleaners in, but you didn't come here to talk about the house, come into the drawing room, there are some things you ought to see. Please sit down, Mr Martin, and I'll get them.'

Ethel Adams walked over to a large walnut desk and, opening a drawer, produced a collection of letters held together with a rubber band.

'Take a look at these, chief inspector.'

Ethel Adams handed the letters to Martin who flipped through the bundle. There were about twenty in all and as far as he could see addressed by the same hand.

'They are all in date order, Mr Martin, the earliest about January last year.'

The chief inspector read out loud the earliest in the pile.

"Dear Miss Adams, I am writing to enquire when you are likely to review my book which you agreed to do a few weeks ago. I have been scouring the News Chronicle and other dailies for some while and also the Malvern Gazette but have found nothing. I presume this is an oversight which you will rectify shortly. Yours sincerely, Ronald Marsh."

'Who is Ronald Marsh, Miss Adams?' enquired Martin.

'He's a local budding author who, I gather, wrote a detective story which he presented, indeed forced quite inappropriately, upon my sister at a cocktail party they were both attending in Tewksbury. She was a literary reviewer, you know, and her reviews were published in some national newspapers and also occasionally locally as necessary. This man, according to my sister, got quite the wrong impression that she would publish a favourable review after she wrote to him and agreed to consider the matter despite her initial annoyance. However, she made no commitment that she would publish such a review, favourable or otherwise, and she told him that. In any case, the story really wasn't any good and when Olive demurred, as you will see, Mr Marsh started writing ever more disagreeable letters to the point where my sister became quite upset. The most recent one is really most unpleasant, written only a few days before she was murdered. I suggested she go to a solicitor, perhaps even the police but I don't think she ever did.'

'All right, I think I need to examine these in detail, Miss Adams, so may I take them away? I'll let you have them back as soon as I've finished with them.'

'Of course, but I don't really think I want them back, they're so unpleasant. Do you think that they might have any bearing on my sister's murder?'

'It's too early to say, but I hope so, I'll let you know as soon as I can. By the way, where did you find them? we searched the house when we were up here.'

'In that heavy old desk over there, they were hidden behind one of the drawers. I only found them when I had to move the thing. I think my sister probably wanted to keep the letters away from Mrs Black, the daily help.'

'Did this man Marsh come here?'

'Not as far as I know, if he did, Olive never mentioned it.'

'Do you know where he lives?'

'No, but I suppose he may be in the telephone book.'

'Don't worry, we'll find him, Miss Adams, thanks for your help.'

Back in the office at the station, Martin and his DI carefully studied the letters.

'Not a very pleasant bloke our friend Marsh, is he?' commented Carlsen. 'Seems to have written about one a week. I think we're going to have to have a little chat with him.'

'Agreed,' replied Martin, 'but he doesn't actually threaten Adams with any harm, he's just downright unpleasant. Anyway, we've found his address, so you and I will pay our writer of detective stories a little visit when we've had a cup of tea; somebody get the kettle on.'

'Mr Marsh?' enquired Martin later that day after a bespectacled man answered the door at a house in Albert Road South.

'Yes.'

'My name is Detective Chief Inspector Martin and this is my colleague, Detective Inspector Carlsen from Malvern police, may we have a word, please?'

'Of course, you'd better come in.'

'We're investigating the murder of Miss Olive Adams, sir, and we hope you can help us. We understand you knew Miss Adams, is that correct?'

'Not terribly well, most of our contact was by letter.'

'And mostly from you, it seems,' said the chief inspector, flourishing the package of correspondence.

'Well, yes, they were in connection with my book which she was reviewing.'

'Some of them are rather impolite, sir, wouldn't you agree?' Without waiting for a reply, Martin continued, 'I quote from the last one you wrote a week before she died. "When are you going to stick to your promise? I'm sick of this, the public need to know I've written this book and you are standing in my way, kindly get on with it without further ado. I expect a positive reply by return."

'Hardly well mannered, sir, is it?' Martin asked, staring at the man.

Marsh fidgeted nervously in his chair and looked embarrassed.

'Well, er, no, chief inspector, but I was angry after she kept turning me down; without a fair wind, the chances of getting a book published are so limited.'

'Had a publisher agreed to take your book on?'

'No.'

'Why didn't Miss Adams review it?'

'That's what I wanted to find out, particularly after she said she would do so. Having reviewed it, I'd hoped that she might have some influence with a potential publisher even if only in the local press which would then help it on its way. She had the manuscript, all she had to do was let me know.'

'It's hardly surprising that she didn't after all the abusive letters you sent her,' said Carlsen.

'I have to agree,' admitted Marsh, 'but I rather lost touch with reality. Look, I'm sorry she died but I had nothing to do with her death, which I suppose is the real reason you're here?'

'Did you ever visit her house?' Carlsen continued.

'No.'

'Are you certain, Mr Marsh?'

'Yes, absolutely certain.'

'Because given your animosity towards Miss Adams,' said the DI, 'it's rather natural that you should be near the top of our list of suspects. Did you ever harm her or threaten her in any way?'

Marsh looked alarmed.

'No, I told you, I never went to her house, I never harmed her, I never threatened her.'

'Nevertheless, we would like your fingerprints, please.'

'But why? I already told you that didn't go to the house.'

'I realise that, sir, but we need your fingerprints for elimination purposes at the house. If we believed everything that people told us we'd soon be in a mess.'

'Do I have an option?'

'Yes, but if you don't provide them, we might jump to conclusions as to your involvement in her murder and start making life very difficult for you. So, attend the police station as soon as possible, please, it won't take more than a few minutes.'

'Yes, but I've—oh, very well.'

'All right, Mr Marsh, that will do for the present,' said Martin, 'but don't go away anywhere without telling us first, we may need to speak to you again.'

'Bit of a nasty bastard but I don't really think he's our man, sir, do you? And as far as we know, he hasn't got any previous,' Carlsen commented back in the car.

'I'm inclined to agree, but we'll do a bit of digging into his background see what we can find. Hopefully, his dabs might turn up trumps if not for this, then as a suspect for something else.'

Chapter 14

After the two men had returned to the station, Sergeant White called them aside.

'Sorry to bother you, Mr Martin but I sent one of my PCs around to Jesse Thurrock's address and he showed him the wallet with the photo in but he got a very odd reaction from the man, who denied any knowledge of the picture, even said it wasn't him at first. He said he had no idea who owned the wallet, got quite shirty about it. I've also checked lost property but nothing there.'

'All right thanks, sarge, leave it with me, I'll have a think about that and perhaps pop around there myself.'

'I don't know but everyone keeps ducking and diving at the moment, John,' remarked the chief inspector. 'If only somebody could show me the path to the promised land then we'd get on a whole lot better and we could all retire. Tell you what, whilst having a dig around into Marsh's past, while you're at it do the same on Thurrock. If there's anything interesting, we'll go and have another chat with our quarryman friend.'

'One of the DCs has found something on that Thurrock bloke, sir,' announced Carlsen in the DCI's office early that evening, 'apparently he was done for soliciting some years ago at Leominster. It must be our man, lives at the same address. He's never come to light here as far as I know, but I'm wondering if the owner of that wallet is one of his pansy friends and that's why he's denying any knowledge. But Worcester also know about him, he's been seen in a queers' club in the town. Apparently, the CID had words with him about his behaviour but he's never actually been nicked there. As for Marsh, no previous or anything else known about him so far.'

'OK, leave Marsh for a while until we get his dabs, you never know, they might match something at the Adams's place. If not, he's out of it, I reckon, but I suppose we'd better keep an open mind.

'So, any particular associates of Thurrock that we know of?' the DCI continued.

'Well, could be,' said the DI, 'because lo and behold, one John Perks, who was recently reported missing was rumoured to be one of his mates at the club according to local CID. I've got his details here because Worcester sent them over to us on the printer when his missus said that he often came over to Malvern to walk in the hills. He's a railwayman, works at Worcester railway shed. She seemed to know that he went to a club but professed ignorance about the place; perhaps couldn't face the truth. You never know he could just be the owner of that wallet.'

'OK, I think before we speak to Thurrock again, we should chat to Mrs Perks and see if she can give us some more info on her missing beau. I'll get on to Worcester and tell 'em that we want a visit and we can take the wallet over, minus the photograph, maybe she can identify it. And when we've finished with her, we can go to the engine shed and chat to some of Perks's mates if he had any. Give them a ring, John, and let them know we're coming. On second thoughts, I need to be here tomorrow, you do it and take Roberts with you.'

The following morning, the two men knocked on the door of 25 Railway Lane, Worcester and introduced themselves to Enid Perks.

'I assume there's no sign of your husband yet, Mrs Perks?' the DI enquired.

'No, the local coppers keep calling and asking the same thing, I've no idea where he is.'

'We're sorry he's not turned up yet, but one of the reasons we've come over here is that we'd like you to take a look at this wallet. It was recently found in Malvern and we wonder whether it might have belonged to your husband?'

The woman examined it for a moment.

'Well, I don't know for certain, it could have been I suppose, he always kept it in his coat pocket. One day, he did say that he had lost it and only had a few pence left in his pocket. He was worried that he wouldn't have enough money to last until his next wage packet.'

'Do you remember when that was?'

'No, sorry.'

'What about his friends, Mrs Perks?' Carlsen asked.

'I don't think he had many, like, least ways I never saw none here. He used to go to a club somewhere in the town, don't know nothing about it though.'

'Did you ever go with him?'

'He never would let me, said it weren't the kind of place wives went, like. Look, why are you asking all these questions? I've already told the police as much as I know.'

'Just making sure we've got our facts right, that's all, Mrs Perks,' replied Carlsen, 'we'll leave it at that for now and we hope to have some good news for you soon.'

The woman nodded and closed the door after them. A downstairs curtain twitched as she watched them go down the short path to the road.

'She didn't seem overly distressed about her missing husband, sir,' commented Roberts outside.

'No, she probably realises what he was up to, but it's not surprising she couldn't identify the wallet. He wouldn't have wanted her to see it, not with a picture of some strange bloke inside.'

'All right, we'll walk up to the railway place and see if we can find our way to the foreman's office, he's in charge of the engine cleaners apparently. We've been given directions; the main thing is to avoid being run over by a railway engine.'

'What a horrible job working in these conditions,' commented Roberts as the two men crunched their way over gravel, ash and general grime towards what they hoped was their destination. A thick sulphurous haze hung over the area and the constant sound of engine whistles could be heard, augmented by trains leaving the local railway stations.

'Being a railwayman runs in the generations like going down the pit, my grandfather was an engine driver on the line to Ashchurch and my old man was as well; I thought about it but didn't suit me. Anyway, I'm too tall to be on the footplate.'

'Hey, try not to get run over, Roberts,' interrupted Carlsen as the sergeant came perilously close to a passing locomotive.

'You looking for me?' a man standing nearby called out.

'Are you the cleaners' foreman, Mr Ross?' The detective inspector enquired, shaking the man's hand.

'That's me, glad to see you didn't get run over.'

'Well, it was a close-run thing with my sergeant here,' replied Carlsen.

'I understand you want to know about John Perks, one of our engine cleaners. I've got some of his mates lined up so you can have a chat but I didn't know him much, haven't long been here meself. This way, they're in my office.'

The three men then went into a small room attached to the engine shed, where three men, faces smeared with grime and wearing even grimier overalls waited inside.

Ross introduced his charges.

'This 'ere is Mick Shields, the middle one, Joe Smith and he's Fred Wilkinson. Police to see you, lads, I'll hang around if that's all right.'

'Yes, of course,' replied Carlsen, 'perhaps we could start by me explaining what this is all about. One of your mates, John Perks, disappeared more than a week ago now and we're concerned that something might have happened to him, to say nothing of his missus. How long did you know him?'

The three men exchanged glances.

'Well, I suppose I must have known him the longest, like,' volunteered Fred Wilkinson who was the eldest of the group. 'I've been here a while.'

'How long's that?' Carlsen asked.

'Oh, about seven years, I suppose.'

'And what did you think of him?'

'Well, he wasn't a bad worker, like, was he, lads? Wasn't exactly a ladies' man if you know what I mean.'

The other two men tittered.

'Well, you know, we reckon he was a bit of a pansy, like,' continued Wilkinson.

'Is that just a rumour or do you know that for certain?' Roberts asked.

'Oh, we knew it, all right, John took a shine to a young lad who was a cleaner here, had to leave, he did; John Perks should have been sacked.'

Fred Wilkinson glanced at the foreman.

'Don't look at me, Fred, before my time,' said Ross.

'Did he ever mention any mates away from work?' Roberts continued.

'No,' replied Wilkinson, 'not that we know of, like, let's face it, he didn't have many here either.'

'Have any of you seen this wallet before or the bloke whose picture is inside?' Carlsen asked, passing it around.

There was a shaking of heads.

'All right, thanks, we'll leave it that. But if anyone has any bright ideas as to where we might find John Perks, please tell us.'

'Thanks, Mr Ross, we'll back in touch if necessary.'

Carlsen and Roberts made their way carefully back to the road outside the works where they had left the car. A dusting of smuts from the engine shed lay on the windows and had to be brushed off.

'Just confirms what we already guessed, sir, doesn't it?' the detective sergeant commented.

'Yes, the thing is though, we can't quite link the wallet with Perks. If we could, that would confirm that he and Thurrock were known to each other, of course; trouble is, Worcester CID can't really confirm 100% that they did.'

The car radio suddenly sprang into life and Roberts picked up the mike and acknowledged.

'Message for Detective Inspector Carlsen, Malvern,' said the voice, 'please call at Worcester CID before returning to your station.'

'All right, let's go, Roberts, I wonder what that's about?' Carlsen and Roberts parked the car in the station yard at Worcester police station and went upstairs to the CID office.

'DI Carlsen from Malvern, someone wants to see us,' he announced.

'Yes, that's me,' said DCI Green, emerging from his office.

'Regarding this Perks job, Mr Carlsen, we've had a bloke come into the nick called Michael Finch, reckons he saw Perks outside that queers' club with a man a few days before he disappeared. Says he, Finch, used to work with Perks. Now, he didn't know who the other man was, but if you pop in a picture of Thurrock which we took at the time he was nicked over here amongst some others for evidential purposes, you might strike lucky. Thurrock has probably changed a bit but might be good enough for identification. As Mr Martin said you were over here, it might save you another journey. I've got Finch's address, you might just catch him in. We can loan you a selection of photos.'

'By the way, even though matey went missing on our patch, as you've been doing most of the legwork, I've agreed with your DCI and Mr Fowler that you should take over the enquiry. After all, chummy is probably buried on your patch somewhere, probably drank too much of the Malvern waters.'

The chief inspector guffawed loudly and vanished back into his office.

Having left the police station, Carlsen and Roberts made their way to a little terraced house on the other side of town and banged loudly on the door.

It slowly creaked open and a woman's voice asked loudly, 'Who are you? What do you want?'

Carlsen explained.

'Well, he's in there in the front room,' continued the woman who turned out to be his wife, 'but he's bloody useless, he should be out getting a job instead of sitting on his backside doing nothing and getting under my feet all day.'

The two men introduced themselves to a middle-aged overweight man who was lounging on a shabby sofa with dance music playing in the background.

'Mr Finch, we understand you might be able to help us regarding the disappearance of John Perks from Railway Lane,' ventured Carlsen, 'can you tell us what you know?'

'Well, I knew him once, that's all, used to work with the bloke on the railway until I decided to get another job; I'm out of work now.'

'Have you've seen him recently?'

'Yeah, a couple of days before he disappeared, like.'

'Where was that?'

'Outside that queers' club just off Foregate Street.'

'What? The Red Feather?'

'Yeah, that's the one.'

'And what was he doing?'

'Well, he were chatting to this bloke, if you can call it chatting, like, all lovey dovey, they were.'

'What do you mean?'

'Well, you know, arms around each other, 'nuff to make you sick.'

'Are you sure it was John Perks you saw?'

'Of course, I'm sure, I told you I used to work with him.'

'And what about the other bloke, had you ever seen him before?'

'No, can't say I have, like.'

'Take a look at this wallet,' said Carlsen, having previously removed the photograph, 'can you say whether that belongs to John Perks?

'No, no, I can't.'

'All right, I've got a selection of photographs here. Please have a careful look and tell us whether you can identify anybody. Take your time.'

Finch examined each photograph, carefully placing each one side by side on a low table.

'Yeah, that's him, that's the other bloke John was talking to, like,' he announced after a while, flourishing a photograph from the selection.

'Are you certain that it's the same man you saw outside the Red Feather? It's very important.'

'Yeah, I'm certain.'

'In which case, we'll need a statement from you regarding your identification of both men; we'll take it now if we can.'

'Don't want to in particular, like, but if I have to.'

'It would be very helpful, Mr Finch.'

'Well, that's a bit interesting, sir,' said Roberts when they got back in the car half an hour later. 'I'd say we'd got Thurrock by the short ones, wouldn't you? It's a good job we had that photo.'

'Yep, now that we can prove that the two men know each other, the wallet has to belong to the feller from Worcester, but unfortunately any half decent defence barrister would suggest that it could belong to someone else who just happened to have another wallet with a photo of Thurrock in it, especially if our friend puts it about a bit. But such is police work. The main question is, where the hell is Perks now?'

'And the other thing, sir, is how did the wallet end up in Malvern Priory cemetery?'

'That's another question that needs answering, but the chances are that it was lost somewhere else and found by one of our local thieves who helped himself to the contents and dumped it where it was found by that gardener. I doubt Thurrock had anything to do with it. If he had, he would have burned it or something. But the other thing is, why did Thurrock deny knowing Perks? It might be that he didn't want the homosexual thing to be made public or worse that he's done him in for whatever reason. Anyhow, it might be worth putting it about amongst our snouts that we're interested in where the wallet was originally found. Someone might have been flashing a bit of money about, not that it's likely to have been a fortune on a railwayman's wages; but it might give us a clue as the whereabouts of our missing man.'

Carlsen and Roberts updated DCI Martin back at the station.

'We might have struck gold, sir,' said Carlsen who then explained the details.

'Excellent, we'll see what our snouts have to say before going to see Thurrock.

The other thing is that Marsh has been in and given his dabs for the Adams business so we'll have to wait on that one but I'm not hopeful.'

Two days later, Carlsen sat in his office as Roberts detailed progress on a series of burglaries that had been taking place all over the Pickersleigh Road area.

'Seems to be the same MO, sir, in and out by the back door, no smashed windows, nothing, so not necessarily using a jemmy, but sometimes he just walks in because some people will insist on keeping their back doors unlocked. Never been seen so far, as we know, and always stays well clear of the owners so he must have a good look first before making a move, always on better quality properties. Never operates at night, again as far as we know. No dabs so far, so he's careful.'

'All right, Roberts, keep a couple of DCs on observation, he'll get careless one day and then we'll have him. I don't suppose for one second there's a link with the Adams affair but we must keep an open mind. Certainly, our Pickersleigh friend doesn't employ violence, not so far anyway.'

The phone rang.

'Sir, no luck on those dabs belonging to Ronald Marsh you sent us,' said a voice, 'can confirm that they don't match anything found at that old lady's address and there's nothing else on him.'

'Damn. All right, thanks,' replied Carlsen.

'Anything interesting?' Chief Inspector Martin enquired, sticking his head around the door.

'Worcester's been on the phone, no go on the Marsh dabs, sir, nothing to link him with the Adams murder or anything else come to that.'

'Well, not surprising, so in the absence of any further information coming to light, that's it for the moment, but I'll pass on the news to her sister and she can have the letters back. I've no doubt Mr Fowler will want us to press on regardless but, if so, he can come up with some bright ideas because I haven't got any.'

Chapter 15

The following morning soon after Carlsen had arrived in the office, there was a knock on his door.

'Yes, Empson.'

'Sir, one of my informants reckons he knows of one of our down and outs who's had a bit more money than he usually does. He was flashing it about in the Wyche Inn up the Cutting.'

'Got a name?'

'Yes, sir, Sidney Hawks, a young lad, never held down a proper job, sometimes kips in the Priory churchyard. If it's all right, I'll see if I can find him, he doesn't usually try to keep out of sight too much.'

'OK, but don't nick him, at least not now, I'm more interested in how he got hold of that cash. Handy that he sometimes sleeps in the churchyard as that's where the wallet was found by the gardener.'

'Presumably there were no dabs, sir?'

'Not worth trying, too many people had handled it by the time we realised its importance. But our friend, Hawks doesn't need to know that.'

'Right, I'll get on it, sir.'

That day, it was nearing dusk when Sidney Hawks went into Priory churchyard for the night. He headed for the most sheltered part which was up against a wall behind a large yew tree that dominated the cemetery, for he reckoned it was going to be cold one. He settled down with an old blanket he usually carried with him, which otherwise doubled as an overcoat. The priory church clock had just finished striking ten when a figure suddenly loomed out of the darkness.

'Hello, Sid, just the man I want to see,' said a voice in the gloom.

'Who's there? What do you want?' asked Hawks nervously.

'It's only me, Sid, I want some information.'

'Oh, it's you, Mr Empson, you darn near frightened me to death.'

'What I want to know is what do you know about that wallet that turned up here the other day?'

'What wallet? I don't know about any wallet,' replied the man.

'Oh, I think you do, you know better than to start telling porkies to me, Sid, because you know what happens to people who tell me fibs. Now, let's start again. A wallet was found here by the gardener a few days ago and my guvnor is interested in knowing where it came from; it's got prints all over it and it won't take long to identify them.'

'I know nothin' about it.'

'See this?' The detective said.

'What?'

Empson clenched his fist.

'This is what you're going to get unless you help me out, because I don't want to upset my guvnor. Now, if you're a good boy, there's a couple of bob in it for you and you won't get nicked. Comprenez?'

'What?'

'Do you understand?' the detective replied loudly.

'All right, Mr Empson, I needed the money, nobody else is going to look out for me, are they?'

'Where did you find it, Sid?'

'Up at the quarry.'

'Which quarry?'

'Thurrock's.'

'Where precisely?'

'It were just off the footpath in some long grass, like, close to that old hut; I'd sleep there given the chance but it's usually locked.'

'How much money was there?'

'Ten and six.'

'Where did you spend it?'

'Most of it in the Wyche, like.'

'You ought to try getting a job, Sid, then you wouldn't get yourself into trouble. So, was it you that dumped the wallet in the cemetery?'

'Yeah.'

'Was there anything else in it, like an address or something?'

'No, just a picture of some bloke, that's all.'

'Recognise him?'

'No, why should I?'

'By the way, don't you ever take a bath, Sid? Christ, you stink.'

'Where am I going to find a bath, Mr Empson, St Ann's Well?'

'Anyway, we're interested in finding the person who owns that wallet,' continued the detective, 'so keep your nose to the ground and also if you see the bloke in the wallet let us know, Sid, nice talking to you.'

'But what about a few bob, Mr Empson? You promised. I've just given you some information.'

'Look, you've just spent ten shillings and sixpence of someone else's money, what more do you want?'

And with the that the detective vanished into the gloom.

'Miserable bastard,' muttered Hawks under his breath but he was glad to see the detective go.

'Had some luck, sir,' reported Empson to DI Carlsen later at the station, 'found Hawks in the cemetery as he was about to have a kip, admits nicking and dumping that wallet; found it near that old hut up at Thurrock's quarry. He says there was a ten and a six in it which, of course, he's spent. But didn't know the name of the bloke in the photo, no reason to think he's lying about that, he's got nothing to gain by it. Didn't nick him as instructed, sir, probably just as well as he'd stink the charge room out.'

'All right, well done, Empson. Next stop, Mr Thurrock, but right now I'm ready for home otherwise my wife'll think I've run off with someone.'

The following morning, Carlsen had a discussion with Martin.

'So, what have we got?' Martin asked and then, answering his own question, continued: 'Well, we've got a missing person, a wallet with a photograph, and Thurrock, who firstly denied it was him in it, plus saying he doesn't know Perks and a tramp who's nicked a few bob. Trouble is, as things stand at the moment, the best we can hope for is Thurrock admitting he's a queer for all the good that will do. Otherwise, we're a bit stuck up a gum tree at the moment, but another visit to our friend is certainly in order; he must know more than he's telling us.'

Chapter 16

'Before we start anything else, what do you make of Empson, John?' Martin asked the following morning in a theatrical whisper meanwhile getting up and closing the office door, 'he hasn't been here long, has he?'

'A bit longer than you, sir, actually, a year or two, I'd say. He's got a bit of a history, none too kind to prisoners at times. Apparently, he nearly got the tin tack when he was a PC at Kidder, started pushing an elderly woman about in the charge room who was a bit stroppy and who'd been nicked for shoplifting. She was never charged with anything, which left the skipper out on a limb a bit. It was only because she didn't want to pursue it that Empson didn't receive a formal complaint. But he got unofficial words of advice, not least from the sergeant, but not formal discipline. Rumour had it that he only saved his job because he was distantly related to the chief constable. I don't know whether that's true or not, but he seems to have behaved himself since he arrived here and turns in the work. Being a bit older, the younger DCs tend to look up to him, which may or may not be a good thing. Sorry, sir, I should have mentioned his history before.'

'It doesn't matter, but I'll tell you why I ask,' said Martin. 'I've had yet another call from the guvnor, but instead of chivvying me on the Adams murder, he started talking about Empson. Apparently, about three years ago, an old boy called Fred Green over at Kidderminster was visited by a bloke purporting to be a detective who was after some information on the old man's son who was wanted for a series of breakings. Now, the story goes that the man was unable or possibly unwilling, to give any information and the detective smacked him one. The man then fell over and, hitting his head on a door, collapsed. Allegedly, the DC left him lying there, didn't even call an ambulance. He was only found by his daily who called around later in the day. The bloke told his tale to this woman and then promptly kicked the bucket. So, basically, County have an unsolved murder on their books with a bit of a fog swirling around Empson.'

'I've heard the rumours about that job but not the detail or the Empson link before,' responded the DI, 'no names, just that CID were involved.'

'Well, it seems that Empson, even though it was his enquiry, denied ever having been at the address, certainly at the time of the assault, and there were no witnesses, no dabs, nothing. It was only when the old man's daily had to go into the nick on some other matter a few months later that she happened to speak to Empson and the name rang a bell. It seems that the name had been mentioned to her by the dying man but couldn't definitely make out what it was at the time. The DC only ever admitted to having spoken to the dead man on the phone, so maybe that's what prompted the victim to come up with Empson's name before he croaked.'

'That sounds a bit farfetched, sir, doesn't it? The woman would be eaten alive by the defence at any trial, especially as she heard his name again at the nick.'

'Yes, quite probably, but be that as it may, it's the situation as described to me by Mr Fowler. There doesn't seem to be sufficient evidence to investigate Empson, so I think it's just a question of keeping an eye on him, although why at this particular time, I don't know. Maybe there's something Mr Fowler's not telling us. No need to mention it to Roberts or anyone else, although it's quite probable that rumours have been flying about the office, you know what the job's like. But the fewer people who know officially the better.'

'Agreed, sir. I worked with Empson; he was on my relief for a while when I was temporarily a uniform inspector at Kidder. He was a good copper, but if anyone got nicked for assaulting police, it was invariably him who was the arresting officer and he had a quick temper. The other blokes used to avoid getting involved with any of his cases if they could, didn't want to be dropped in it. I also heard on the grapevine, although I've no evidence of it, that Empson was a bit light fingered with other people's property.'

'Yes, well, we'll see what happens, just keep a weather eye, that's all.'

Chapter 17

'Come on, John, in the car, time to visit our friend, Thurrock, again,' said Martin the following morning. 'I think we'll give the impression that the wallet definitely belongs to Perks and we've got Finch's identification of Thurrock to back us up. Anyway, we can wave it at him at the appropriate time and see what he says.'

In due course, the two men banged on the door of The Grange, the butler answered and Martin and Carlsen introduced themselves.

'I don't think you're expected, are you, gentlemen?' the man queried.

'No, but it's important.'

There was a short pause before the butler returned.

'Come in, officers, Mr Thurrock will see you now.'

The two men were then conducted to a small side room off the hallway.

'Not good enough for the drawing room, are we?' Carlsen muttered to Martin as they waited.

'No, and nor is he come to that,' the other responded.

The man soon appeared.

'We're sorry to trouble you again, Mr Thurrock,' said the DCI, 'but we're investigating the disappearance of a Mr John Perks. You may recall one of our officers called recently and talked to you about a wallet that turned up locally.'

'Yes, but I was unable to help at the time and I told the officer that.'

'But we think you can help,' said Martin. 'You see, there's the question of the photograph in the wallet, you denied knowing the identity of the wallet's owner but we think you know who it is.'

'Oh, why's that?'

'Because we have a witness who says that he saw you in the company of a John Perks, whom we've established owns the wallet, and your photo is definitely inside even though you initially denied it to the officer who first came around to see you.'

'Well, your witness has made a mistake.'

'We think not, Mr Thurrock, you were seen outside the Red Feather club in Worcester in the company of Mr Perks, and what's more the witness once worked with the missing man so there's no mistake.'

'I really can't help you,' insisted the man.

'Stop wasting our time, Mr Thurrock, it's quite clear from the witnesses observations of you and the location that you're a homosexual, it's no good trying to deceive us. And the evidence also indicates that Perks was of the same inclination; we're right, aren't we?'

Thurrock stared into space for a moment then said quietly, 'You're judging me, chief inspector, so I am of a certain inclination, to use your words, that's the way things are, having draconian laws on the statute book will not stop me from behaving the way I do. And yes, I do know John Perks and we enjoy each other's company.'

'We're not here to discuss the rights and wrongs of the law, Mr Thurrock, we're investigating a missing person or possibly worse. Now, what do you know about the disappearance of this man?'

'Nothing, we used to meet from time to time, occasionally at the club in Worcester and also up at the quarry where we used to walk sometimes. That's all I can tell you.'

'How long have you been friends?'

'A lot of years.'

'When did you last see him?' Carlsen asked.

'Oh, a few weeks ago.'

'And did you part on amicable terms?'

'Yes, perfectly.'

'I ask you again, Mr Thurrock,' persisted Martin, 'are you certain that you don't know the whereabouts of John Perks?'

'Absolutely positive.'

'All right, did he give any indication that he might be considering disappearing from sight or going somewhere else?'

'No.'

'And this wallet, Mr Thurrock, does it belong to Mr Perks?' Martin asked.

The man glanced at it.

'Yes, all right, I think it does, although how he lost it, I don't know, he never mentioned it; sweet of him to keep my photo though.'

'That will do for the moment,' said Martin, 'don't leave Malvern without telling us where you're going, Mr Thurrock, we may need to interview you again.'

'Unconvincing bastard, isn't he, sir?' Carlsen remarked on the way back to the station.

'Yes,' said Martin, 'but we've no real evidence that he knows anything about Perks's fate, but I'd bet my pension he does. If he has killed the man over some lover's tiff or whatever, it's likely to be away from his home what with the butler and all that. Certainly doesn't seem to have a wife. So, what next, John?'

'How about starting at the quarry, sir?' suggested Carlsen.

'Yes, how about that for a good idea? Tell you what, we'll go up there mob handed in the morning and have a sniff about, we can't lose anything. And bring a screwdriver and jemmy, we might need to do a bit of hut breaking. Better get a warrant though just to cover our backs.'

'What about Thurrock, shall we get him up there?'

'No, let him sweat, John, we can always arrange a nice little visit if necessary.'

Chapter 18

The following day, Martin, Carlsen, Roberts and two DCs walked along the path to Thurrock's quarry as rain threatened but it was quite warm.

'I don't know, sir, but it's always raining or threatening rain whenever I come up here,' remarked Roberts, 'either that or it's bloody freezing cold.'

'Well, if we get wet or freeze to death Roberts, we'll blame you,' commented Carlsen, 'it must be that Upton water that soaks into you when the Severn floods.'

'Thanks very much, sir,' replied the sergeant, grinning.

The men soon arrived at the hut which was locked.

'Looks like the hasp has been replaced but the padlock looks the same,' commented the DI.

'All right, let's have a look then,' instructed the chief inspector, handing over the jemmy, 'get her open, DC Jones.'

The detective constable then jemmied open the door.

'Cor, a bit musty in here, sir,' Roberts sticking his head around the door.

'A bit more than musty, I think,' replied Martin, 'it's downright unpleasant.'

The floor of the hut was mostly covered with a thick layer of dust, but at the far end to the right of the door, there was less dust and Roberts noticed that the ground appeared to have been disturbed.

'Take a look at this, sir, looks as if someone has been messing about here.'

'Well, I wonder what we've got here then?' Martin asked, exchanging glances with Carlsen. 'Jones, get off up to one of those cottages at the end of the path and ask whether we can borrow a spade or a shovel. If there's no one in, use the car radio and get a couple up from the nick.'

Five minutes later, DC Jones returned, spade in hand.

'The bloke in No 2 leant it, sir, glad to know he's doing his bit.'

'All right, get digging, young man,' instructed Carlsen, 'might be treasure down there.'

But it wasn't long before the stench of rotting flesh assailed everyone's nostrils, Jones started to heave as he staggered back dropping the spade.

'OK, outside, lad, get some air,' instructed Carlsen.

'I'll carry on, sir,' volunteered Roberts, tying a handkerchief around his face.

After a little further work, a rotting human carcass was soon revealed with items of clothing embedded in the flesh which was heaving with maggots.

'All right, DC Davies,' instructed Martin, 'go to the car and get on the radio, organise Worcester, photographs, dabs, coroner's officer etc. John, you go with him, give Chief Inspector Rogers my compliments and request some uniform PCs, we're going to be here quite a while. After that, go to Thurrock's house, nick him and bring him up here, we'll see if he can talk his way out of this one.'

Thirty minutes later, Carlsen and Davies appeared through the rainy mist accompanied by a reluctant Jesse Thurrock.

'Ah, Mr Thurrock, I expect DI Carlsen has explained why we want to talk to you. Come into the hut, we've dug up a dead body, a nice ripe specimen, in fact, and we think you can tell us who it is.'

Thurrock hung back.

'What's the matter, Thurrock, don't want to visit an old beau? Now get in there.'

The man stumbled as Martin pushed him through the door, but recovering his balance began to retch violently. He backed out of the hut, gasping for air and sat down hard on the pathway, pale and shaking.

'Not very pleasant, eh? Now, what do you know about our buried friend in there? But before you answer, I'm obliged to remind you that you're under caution.'

'Nothing, nothing at all,' replied the man, eventually recovering his composure.

'Oh, don't be silly, Mr Thurrock. You know, as well as I do, who that is in there, it's John Perks, unless of course it's the man from Mars.'

'I told you, I know nothing about it, I want my solicitor.'

The chief inspector groaned.

'All right, we're going to have to do this the hard way. You will now be taken down to the police station and you can stew in a nice comfy cell until we're good and ready to talk. And on the way, we're going to search your house.'

'You can't do that,' protested Thurrock.

'Really? We beg to differ, don't worry, you'll have a grandstand view,' said the DCI.

Martin spoke to Roberts.

'You and Davies stay here until the boys from Worcester arrive and I'll check that the nick is sending up some uniform. Jones, you come with us. The coroner's officer should arrive in due course closely followed by the undertakers. Boy, are they going to love this one!

'So, block off the path at both ends when you can and nobody else comes along here or goes in the hut without your authority, sarge. It may be that the pathologist will want to visit. Anyway, Mr Carlsen or I will come back later on and wrap things up. All right?'

'Sir,' Roberts acknowledged.

Thurrock was then taken to the police car, which after a short while, pulled up in the driveway of "The Grange".

'We're after anything that confirms his link with Perks, John, but I'll be surprised if we find anything,' whispered Martin as they walked through the front door which had been opened by the butler, mouth agape. Thurrock who was handcuffed lead the way.

The house was then searched but, as expected, nothing was found.

Back at the station, having put Thurrock into a cell, Martin and Carlsen sat and waited over a cup of tea for the prisoner's solicitor to arrive.

'Well, sir, what do you reckon?' Carlsen asked.

'We should have him bang to rights but he could make a fight of it. But there's no sign of any forced entry to the hut or anyone else tampering with the lock before we arrived. I suppose he could claim that someone else killed Perks and put him in there, but I don't think a jury would buy that one, which brings into play the question of keys. Who has access to the hut apart from Thurrock? Anyhow, I reckon he had a spat with his boyfriend and welted him one. Whether he intended to kill him or not, we'll have to wait and see; either way given a fair wind, it'll be at least manslaughter.'

'Solicitor here, sir,' called Sergeant White from the top of the stairs.

'My word, Mr Stevens, you are a busy man,' commented DCI Martin, on seeing a familiar figure at the front counter. 'I explained the circumstances to you over the phone, so I won't go over them again but we intend to interview Mr Thurrock under caution and see where we get to. So, can we start as soon as possible, please?'

Thurrock was escorted into the interview room and was left with his solicitor for a short consultation.

Five minutes later, the prisoner and Stevens were joined by Martin and Carlsen.

'Mr Thurrock, I remind you that you are still under caution,' said Martin.

The suspect nodded but stared at the table and said nothing.

'I want to question you regarding the death of Mr John Perks of Worcester whose body we believe we found today in your hut up at Thurrock's quarry. Have you anything to say about that?'

Thurrock shook his head.

'Are you certain?'

Thurrock glanced at his solicitor but still did not answer.

'Was Mr Perks a friend of yours?' Martin asked.

'You know perfectly well he was,' replied the suspect.

'Remind me how long had you known each other?'

'Oh, probably nearer twenty years than ten.'

'And you met at the Red Feather Club in Worcester?'

'Yes.'

'How often did you meet?'

'Oh, about every couple of weeks or so.'

'And where else did you meet?'

'As I've said before, mostly up at the quarry.'

'So, was your last meeting there?'

'Yes.'

'Specifically where?'

'By the hut.'

'Do you know how Perks got to Malvern that day?'

'By train, he didn't have a car and didn't often use the bus. I usually picked him up at the station, but on this occasion he walked up to the quarry.'

'What date was that meeting?'

'I don't remember precisely.'

'But did you make arrangements to meet again?'

'Yes.'

'Where?'

'At the railway station and then we were planning to go to the quarry.'

'What was your reaction when he failed to turn up?'

'I thought he'd missed the train or was ill or something.'

'Did you try to contact him?'

'No, I didn't know where, I didn't have his address.'

'But you knew he worked on the railway at Worcester?'

'Yes, but the engine shed is a big place, I didn't know what he did there.'

'All right, Mr Thurrock, back to the present. How often do you visit the quarry for business reasons?'

'Oh, about once a week, I suppose.'

'And what do you do up there?'

'Check the quarry to make sure that the pathways are safe for people to use.'

'What about the hut? How often do you go in there?'

'Not every time I visit.'

'But most times when you met Perks?'

'Yes, so what?'

'How many keys are there to the padlock on the hut?'

'That's naughty, chief inspector, you're trying to catch me out.'

'How many keys are there, Mr Thurrock?' repeated Martin.

'Two, I've got one and John has the other.'

'Any others?'

'No, but that doesn't mean to say other people couldn't get in, the lock's not complicated.'

'And where is Perks's key?'

'On his body, I suppose.'

'Oh, so you acknowledge that the body in your hut is that of John Perks?'

'You implied it at the beginning of the interview and after you dragged me up to the quarry. Anyone could have put his body in there.'

Martin and Carlsen exchanged glances.

'Oh, come on, Mr Thurrock,' Martin continued, 'use your brains, you know perfectly well that the chances of somebody else putting Perks' body in YOUR hut, the body of somebody you knew well without being discovered, are minimal. I mean, all this nonsense about making arrangements to meet again, he was already dead because you'd killed him at or near the hut. That's true, isn't it?'

Thurrock said nothing.

'Did you kill John Perks?' persisted Martin.

'No.'

'You see, I think you got rid of Mr Perks because he was going to the police to spill the beans over your relationship or tell his wife. Was he threatening to break off the friendship with you after all those long years of suffering from a guilty conscience? Couldn't stand the pressure of being different anymore, perhaps?'

Jesse Thurrock stared straight at Martin but, again, remained silent.

'Will you give us a statement under caution detailing your actions, Mr Thurrock?' Martin continued.

'I think my client has said all he wishes, chief inspector,' interrupted his solicitor, 'I don't think anything will be gained by it. He has not admitted any offence relating to Mr Perks.'

'Sergeant White,' called Martin, 'take this man down to the cell and I'll arrange for one of my DCs to sit outside; but put a PC on there for the moment.'

'Yes, sir.'

'Mr Stevens, will you wait a moment, please?'

'I think we have to charge him, John,' said Martin in his office. 'I don't think there's anything to be gained by delaying things. The fact that only Thurrock and Perks had a key, I think, clinches it even with that simple lock. So, unless Perks unlocked the door, did himself in, dug his own grave and then re-locked the place from the inside, I don't see that Thurrock has an answer. The other key will probably turn up on Perks' body. It will be interesting to know what the pathologist has to say as to how he died. And why did Thurrock kill the man in the first place? But if it didn't happen for the reasons that I suggested in the interview, then I'm a Dutchman.'

'Or a Swede,' suggested Carlsen.

'Yes, all right, or a Swede, John,' agreed the DCI shooting him a glance, 'but that remark will cost you a pint.'

'Right, sir, I'll arrange with Inspector Pritchard to charge him.'

Thirty minutes later, in the presence of his solicitor, Thurrock was charged with the murder of John Perks.

'Right, John, we'd better go back up to the quarry and see what's happening. No peace for the wicked, eh?'

They were met by Sergeant Roberts at the hut.

'All done, sir, the pathologist himself turned up but won't have much to say until he's examined the body in the mortuary. The coroners officer has had a look and Perks has been moved by the undertakers. They looked a little green by the time they'd finished. Oh, and they found this on his wedding finger, sir,' said the Sergeant producing a gold ring from his pocket.

'Yes, it's Perks' all right,' said Martin, examining the ring, on which the letters 'EP' were visible. 'His missus, Enid, told Worcester that he wore a wedding ring and that it was marked with her initials. She's going to love identifying him on the slab.'

'Poor cow. Anyway, dabs and photos all finished, Roberts?' Carlsen queried.

'Yes, sir, the blokes have just gone. Frank Coles, the coroner's officer, said that the pathologist's report will probably be ready tomorrow. Apparently, two sets of prints were found in the hut, sir, hopefully they'll belong to just Thurrock and Perks. And they also took prints off his fingers, what's left of 'em, so that ought to help. Also, a key turned up in Perks's pocket which fits the padlock on the door.'

'Good, just what I wanted to hear. OK, re-open up the path,' instructed Martin, 'no point in keeping people out now, but I've no doubt the press and the ghouls will want to come up and photograph the place. No point in trying to stop them but we'll keep a couple of PCs here for the time being otherwise they'll start trying to break into the place to get photographs. We need to get a new hasp and decent padlock to keep them out after we're gone; the Council can do that.'

'Meanwhile, gentlemen,' said Martin, 'I think we can all go down the pub. Good job done, but I'd better have a word with the guvnor first, tell him the good news. Also better issue a preliminary statement to the press, we'll stage a full conference tomorrow morning.'

Chapter 19

'The press are baying at the front counter with Miss Davies heading the pack, sir,' said Inspector Carlsen on the following morning.

'All right,' replied the DCI, 'tell 'em there'll be a press conference in an hour, they can sweat for a while. When we take Thurrock to court, they can all rush around there and then rush back here again.'

Later that morning, the prisoner was taken to the court and remanded in custody and then the DCI faced the usual cacophony from the press.

Twenty-four hours passed and Martin received a phone call in his office.

'Detective chief inspector, this is the pathologist,' said a voice, 'I found something interesting on that body you gave me yesterday, I think you ought to come over and take a look.'

'Sounds interesting, John, you'd better come with me, and while we're at it, we can check out the results of the prints that were found in the hut.'

Some while later, Martin and Carlsen parked the car and walked up the steps of Worcester mortuary to be greeted by Rush, the pathologist.

'Good morning, gentlemen, step this way.'

The men were conducted into the inner sanctum where an assistant busied himself pulling the body on a slide out of a protective cabinet.

'This what I found on your specimen,' the pathologist announced, reaching into the drawer of a table that lay to one side of the room.

'It's a letter, Mr Martin, which I found in the breast pocket of the jacket on the body. Its badly stained but just about readable, take a look at it.'

Martin turned over the sheet in his hand and read it out loud.

'Dear sir, if you are reading this, I have been done in by my friend, Jess Thurrock, cos I told him that I were going to the coppers. He has threatened me for years and I would not stand for it no more. It were that young woman he killed that made me realise how bad he was. I wanted to speak before and he's killed me for it. I am sorry that it took very long. It was bad of me. J. Perks.'

The DCI looked incredulous.

'What the hell does he mean, John, what woman? Not another one up at the quarry, surely?'

'Search me, sir,' responded Carlsen shrugging, 'but it certainly can't be Olive Adams, she was anything but young, so there can't possibly be a link.'

'How long has he been in the ground, sir?' Carlsen asked the pathologist.

'Oh, about a couple of weeks. We've had one or two warm days so decomposition is quite advanced, especially in the cooped-up environment of that hut; the maggots have been having a wonderful time. He was strangled, by the way.'

'Well, what do we make of it, sir?' Carlsen remarked, staring at the letter.

'I wish I knew, John, but it's worrying, because as far as I know, we've got no outstanding female missing persons on the books.'

'On the bright side, sir, at least that letter is additional evidence against Thurrock, doesn't give him much room for manoeuvre. And it's proof positive that Thurrock killed Perks because he was threatening to talk to us, it's enough to hang him.'

'True, but let's go and check out those prints,' suggested Martin as they left the mortuary, 'we can also arrange for the letter to be photographed, we'll need it when we talk to our quarryman friend.'

The fingerprints having been confirmed as those of Thurrock and Perks and the letter passed to the photographer, Martin and Carlsen returned to Malvern.

'Sergeant Roberts, in here, please,' called the DI.

'Sarge, I want you to check out all outstanding female missing persons in the county, say from the last ten years, use one of the DCs to help you and you'd better check out Herefordshire as well. I'll speak to the uniform superintendent over there to clear it.'

'Problems, sir?'

'Yes, Perks left a letter in which he accuses Thurrock of murdering a woman but we don't know who that might be. There's no one on our books that fits the bill so that's why we need that misper information. I don't suppose it'll be long before Mr Fowler puts in an appearance looking for answers. So, I need that information as quick as you can.'

The phone rang almost immediately.

'Talk of the devil, John, Mr Fowler is on his way, Worcester have just been on to the switchboard. We'll have to give him the bad news about that letter.'

'Well, at least Thurrock is not going anywhere, sir, we've got time yet.'

'Just as well, this is going to need a visit to Worcester prison, but if Thurrock doesn't co-operate, it could be a tricky one unless Roberts comes up with a missing person that fits the bill. Also, we need to organise Enid Perks to formerly identify her husband, which will be anything but pleasant; I'll leave that to you, John.'

Half an hour later, familiar, heavy footsteps could be heard tramping up the stairs.

'Well done, Mr Martin,' the detective superintendent said jovially after arriving in the office and tossing his hat on the table, 'a good job by everybody.'

'Yes, but I'm afraid the news is not all good, sir.'

The chief inspector explained about the letter.

'Well, that's a turn up, what's happening about that then?'

'DS Roberts is trawling through missing persons' records around the county and also Hereford to see if we can get a match, but I'm not holding out too much hope at this stage. Theoretically, the victim could have come from anywhere. We don't think it's Olive Adams, as the murdered woman is described by Perks in his letter as "young", although we don't know what time period he is referring to as we don't know when he wrote the letter; it's undated. Obviously, we have to arrange a visit to Worcester prison to re-interview Thurrock about this woman, but as we've only just heard about this supposed other murder, I haven't done that yet.'

'All right, keep me informed, Mr Martin, let's hope Thurrock coughs on this one before he hangs for the Perks killing. We don't want an outstanding murder on the books.'

After Fowler's eventual departure, Martin got on the phone and then spoke to DI Carlsen.

'John, I've arranged for us to visit Worcester prison and interview Thurrock at 10 a.m. tomorrow. I've no doubt he'll want his solicitor to be present, so I've let Stevens know as a matter of courtesy, although that's up to the Prison Governor. I hope they've managed to photograph that letter so we can pick it up in the morning on the way to the prison. Any news from Roberts yet?'

'Sarge, what news?' Carlsen called.

'Nothing yet, sir, getting people to check the paperwork is taking time.'

'All right, keep at it, we need to know today. If you're experiencing delaying tactics, let me know, I'm sure Mr Martin will speak to Mr Fowler to speed things up.'

Later in the afternoon, the DS knocked on Carlsen's door. The news was not good.

'No joy, sir, no missing females in our county or Herefordshire that haven't been accounted for. There's nothing that could possibly match going back ten years. Before that, the records simply don't exist anymore unless foul play was suspected, like Miss Sweet.'

Carlsen sighed.

'OK, you've done your best, I'll tell Mr Martin. It looks like we're going to have to rely on Thurrock spilling the beans on what woman Perks was talking about when we produce that letter, which is all right but it would have been useful to have had something definite to hit him with.'

Chapter 20

Shortly before 10 a.m. the following day, Martin and Carlsen rang the bell at the gates of Worcester prison and were ushered into an interview room where Stevens, the solicitor, greeted them. A few moments later, Thurrock appeared accompanied by a prison officer, keys jangling from his belt, who stood in one corner slab-faced and inscrutable with arms folded.

'I'm sure Mr Stevens has told you why we are here, Mr Thurrock,' said Martin, 'but just in case there is any doubt, we are not here in connection with the Perks murder, that awaits the law to take its course, but we are now investigating the murder of another woman and we think that you may be able to assist us. Before we start, however, Detective Inspector Carlsen will caution you.'

Carlsen did as requested but Thurrock remained silent.

'Have you got anything to say to us about your involvement in the murder of a woman not previously discussed, either in Malvern or elsewhere?'

Thurrock shook his head.

'I which case, I want you to look at this photograph of a letter which was written by John Perks and which was found by the pathologist on the body in Worcester mortuary.'

Martin pushed the letter over the table with a copy to Stevens. Thurrock picked it up and read it slowly.

'Don't know anything about it, chief inspector,' Thurrock replied, shaking his head, 'he must have made it up.'

'Why would he do that?'

'Because he was a pathetic little man that's why, he wouldn't have known the truth if somebody kicked him up the arse with it,' the man replied irritably.

'Do you know the truth when you see it, Mr Thurrock?' Martin asked, 'Perks would not have had a motive to implicate you in another murder unless you had committed one. After all, you were long-term friends. The letter was not intended to be seen by anyone unless he, Perks, was already dead and he most certainly is.'

'You're entitled to your opinion,' responded the man shrugging.

'Why are you continuing to lie? You're probably going to hang anyway, at least you should have the decency to explain who this woman is that Perks refers to in the letter.'

Thurrock gave a long look at Stevens followed by a deep sigh. He tapped his fingers on the table for a moment.

Then: 'I want a word with my solicitor alone, please.'

After a few moments' delay, the solicitor asked the two officers to return.

'All right, Mr Detective,' said Thurrock,' I don't quite know why I should be helping the law but you'd better take a look at this.'

Thurrock rummaged in his pocket and, pulling out a shiny object, pushed it across the table to the chief inspector.

'Recognise that Mr Detective?' he asked.

Martin put on his glasses and turned it over in his hand. It was a heavily tarnished, silver clasp. He immediately recognised it but was deeply puzzled.

'Where did you find this, Mr Thurrock?' he asked quietly.

'Well, I suppose finding it is one way of putting it.'

Martin glanced at Carlsen still puzzled.

'What do you mean by that?'

'The penny still hasn't dropped, has it, Mr Detective?'

Martin and Carlsen looked aghast.

'Are you telling us that you were involved in the disappearance of Dorothy Sweet?' continued Martin incredulously.

'Oh, well done, because, yes, yes I am,' smirked Thurrock, 'that's put the cat amongst the pigeons, hasn't it?' Arrested the wrong person, haven't you? Hah, hah. And not only that the woman topped herself because of it, oh dear what a cockup. Bang goes your pension, Martin, and yours too, Mr Detective Inspector.'

The solicitor sat, frozen like a statue as both detectives squirmed inside but remained outwardly impassive.

'This interview is temporarily suspended,' growled Martin, 'we'll restart in a few minutes. A word, Mr Stevens, please.'

They talked in the corridor outside.

'I assure you I had no idea this eventuality was going to occur, gentlemen,' said the solicitor, 'but I'm sure you'll want to get this interview finished as soon as possible.'

'Yes,' replied the chief inspector, 'but please give us a couple of minutes to discuss this new development.'

'God Almighty, what's going on, John?' Martin said after the solicitor was out of earshot. 'Surely, Leticia Glass committed that murder not bloody Thurrock. I can't believe my ears. What about the evidence given by the Austen woman?'

'Good question, sir, but that's for later, now I think we'd better go back in the room and get this finished.'

The two men returned.

'Right, in view of what you said we need to go through this in detail, Mr Thurrock, so that we have a record of the exact sequence of events.'

'The floor is yours, chief inspector,' replied Jesse Thurrock expansively, 'I have all the time in the world until the hangman comes calling.'

'Where were you on the evening of 16 June 1920, the day Miss Sweet disappeared, say between the hours of about 8.0 p.m. and about 10.0 p.m.?'

'Up at my quarry.'

'Thurrock's quarry?'

'Yes.'

'Why were you up there?'

'To meet John.'

'John Perks?'

'Yes.'

'For what purpose?'

'Why do you think?'

'Just answer the question.'

'Sex.'

'What time did he turn up?'

'I don't remember precisely, it was a long time ago, but probably about 8:15 p.m.'

'Where did this encounter take place?'

'In the hut.'

'Did you see anyone else up there?'

'The headmistress woman.'

'Dorothy Sweet?'

'Yes, but I didn't learn the name until later when I saw her picture in the paper.'

'All right, we'll talk about her in a minute.'

'Did you see anyone else apart from Miss Sweet?'

'There was a woman walking along the quarry path, which given the thundery weather and the time of day, I thought quite surprising.'

'Can you describe her?'

'Oh, youngish, probably about twenty; blonde I think but it was a bit gloomy.'

'Which direction was she walking in?'

'From the direction of the road, you know the end where the cottages are, I think she lived in one of them because I thought I'd seen her before more than once.'

'Was John Perks with you at the time?'

'Yes.'

'And were you near the hut when you saw her?'

'Yes, we were just standing there chatting and she walked by?'

'Did you speak to her or her to you?'

'No.'

'Did you see this girl before or after your encounter with Miss Sweet?'

'Before.'

'And did you see the girl again?'

'No.'

'What happened after the woman walked by?'

'We went into the hut.'

'All right, how did Miss Sweet become involved in the situation?'

'John and I were doing things when suddenly the door opened.'

'What happened then?'

'I turned around and there was this woman standing there. You should have seen her face.'

'What happened then.'

'She started shouting, "you dirty, filthy animals," over and over again.'

'So, what did you do next?'

'I pushed her backwards out of the door and she stumbled and I grabbed her and put my hand over her mouth to try and stop her shouting. The clasp on the handle of her handbag broke and fell on the path and suddenly she slipped and disappeared backwards over the edge of the quarry. I looked over the edge but couldn't see her.'

'All right, what then?'

'John was panicking and wanted to call an ambulance but I said "no".'

'Why?'

'Why do you think? I didn't want to end up getting nicked.'

'So, you left this woman to die in the quarry?'

'Well, snooty bitch with all her airs and graces, who was she to walk into my hut and call us animals?'

'You could still have gone for help no matter what she had said, couldn't you? She might still have been alive.'

'I doubt it, there's lots of rocks down that quarry, I didn't hear anything. Anyway, I didn't care much at the time.'

'And what about the clasp, is this the one off her handbag?'

'Yes, I found it on the path.'

'How did it end up here?'

'My ex is clearing out the house because where I'm going, I won't need anywhere to live. She found it in a box, I was going to pawn it but I never got around to it; she brought it in here, didn't realise what it was. The screws weren't going to allow me to keep it but I told 'em that it was a family heirloom and they changed their minds. Trouble is, this place is full of villains, who'd nick the clothes you stood up in if you weren't wearing 'em so I always keep it on me.

'What about the other clasp?' Thurrock asked.

'We've got it.

'All right, what happened to the handbag?' continued the DCI.

'It went over the edge with her.'

'So, after Miss Sweet had gone into the quarry, what did you do next?'

'I picked up the car from the road to the quarry and ran John to the station. As I said, he was in a real panic, kept saying we ought to call an ambulance but I wouldn't allow it.'

'At least, he had a bit of humanity, Mr Thurrock.'

'To hell with humanity, when the chips are down, you've got to look after number one, I say. Over the years, since then he whinged on and off about that woman, how she didn't deserve what happened to her etc. etc. Eventually, I'd had enough when he threatened me with the coppers. Oh, dear, poor John, a bit weak minded. Still, it was fun with him while it lasted. I could tell you more but I won't and you're not allowed to ask me any more questions about John Perks because I've already been charged with his murder. Isn't that right, Mr Stevens?'

The solicitor nodded but looked uncomfortable.

'Are you prepared to give us a statement under caution, regarding Miss Sweet, Mr Thurrock?'

'No, I've said enough.'

The chief inspector rose to his feet.

'After advice and as soon as it can be arranged, you will be charged with the murder of Dorothy Sweet and possibly with other offences, Mr Thurrock,' he said. 'Meanwhile, this interview is concluded.'

'Thank you, Mr Stevens.'

'Thank you, gentlemen,' replied Stevens, 'I shall wait to hear from you, this job is nothing but surprises.'

Chapter 21

'There's no doubt that Thurrock is telling the truth, everything matches, that Austen woman has made a monkey out of us,' said Martin as they returned to the car and drove back to Malvern, 'she must have hated Leticia Glass to pull that kind of trick; I feel responsible, John, I've now got a dead woman on my conscience and nothing is going to change that.'

'Sir, we had to go where the evidence led us and County supported that,' replied Carlsen sympathetically, 'we couldn't ignore what Austen told us. She seemed to be perfectly straightforward and honest, even if the circumstances were a little odd. If anything, she's the one who should have Leticia Glass's death on her conscience.'

'Yes, but she was blonde, pretty, well-spoken and persuasive, John, but I should never have believed her without some corroborative evidence. No wonder she was reluctant to go into the witness box.'

'But if you think back, sir, she mentioned having seen two men on the footpath near the hut, which turned out to be true, so she seemed to have been mixing fact with fiction when she fed us that story.'

'Either way, the cow is coming in when we get back to the nick, I'll drag her in by her pretty blonde hair if needs be. First, though, I'll have to talk to Fowler and break the bad news.'

'I'm sure he'll support you.'

'Yes, well, that probably depends on the attitude of the chief constable.'

Having arrived back in the office, Martin spoke at length on the phone to the detective superintendent.

'How did it go, sir?' Mr Carlsen enquired after the conversation had finished.

'Well, he's not going to hang me quite yet, but as soon as we've interviewed Austen, he naturally wants to know the results. He reckons that there's a good chance of our friend from the quarry being convicted for murdering Perks; hard to disagree with that. As for Sweet, he has his doubts about murder but reckons Thurrock might plead to manslaughter. Even if he doesn't, the jury might believe it was negligence rather than murder if they're given the chance by the judge, and I'm inclined to agree with that. Anyway at the moment, we've got more important fish to fry.

'So, get somebody to go to Worcester, John, and pick up the Austen case papers then we'll get a warrant and interview her.'

Later that day.

'Right, let's get cracking, organise a DC, John, we'll go around and nick Austen now.'

Having knocked loudly at her cottage door at Thurrock's quarry, it was opened by a nervous looking Celia Austen.

'Oh, it's you, Mr Martin and Mr Carlsen, I had a feeling that we might meet again.'

'And why do you think that, Miss Austen?' Martin asked, with just a hint of sarcasm.

'My evidence, I thought you might to talk to me about it.'

'How right you are. Celia Austen, I'm arresting you on suspicion of perjury and I am obliged to caution you. Do you understand?' he asked when he had finished.

'Yes, may I have a solicitor?'

'Of course, you can call one from here if you wish.'

Austen nodded.

'Go with her, John, please, and you too, DC Jones, and then bring her out to the car. She'll need some clothes.'

Back at Malvern police station, Austen sat forlornly in a cell awaiting the arrival of a solicitor, Andrew Logan, who after about an hour, announced his presence at the front counter. After consulting with his client, he declared her ready to be interviewed.

'You take the lead, John,' said Martin as they entered the interview room.

'All right, Miss Austen,' commenced Carlsen, 'you know why you are here, but should there be any doubt, you have been arrested on suspicion of perjury in connection with the arrest and trial of the late Leticia Glass. There is also the matter of making false statements to police. You are still under caution. Do you understand?'

'Yes,' replied the woman, staring at the floor.

The DI shuffled the papers in front of him.

'On 21 August 1937, you came into this police station and told us verbally and then in writing what you alleged you saw on the evening of 16 June 1920 up at Thurrock's quarry. Would you agree that this is the original statement you made to us when you were here?'

Austen examined it carefully, nodded and then passed it over to her solicitor.

'Since that date, the trial of Leticia Glass for the murder of Miss Dorothy Sweet took place, during which Miss Glass committed suicide before its conclusion, we think because she believed she was going to be convicted of murder. Secondly, whilst being investigated on another matter, an individual has indicated that it was he who was responsible for the disappearance of your former headmistress and not Miss Glass. Do you understand?'

'Yes, yes, I do.'

'As the trial was triggered by your evidence, please explain why you lied to us.'

'I, I don't know,' the woman answered falteringly, 'it was insane, stupid, I don't know what came over me.'

'I need a more detailed answer than that, Miss Austen,' said the detective inspector.

'Well, I suppose it all started back at the college. That hateful woman made my life a misery throughout my stay at the school, and not only me, she bullied other girls, especially those whom she particularly disliked and there were plenty of those. Even when I was appointed head girl, not much changed, she just had it in for me, I think possibly because she may have objected to my appointment but been overruled by Miss Sweet.'

'You mentioned in your first statement that you and other girls had suffered punishment at the hands of Miss Glass. Did you go to the headmistress and complain about Miss Glass's behaviour?'

'No, it was not the sort of thing you did, it would have been seen as a cry-baby thing to do.'

'What about your parents, surely they would have been sympathetic?'

'Possibly or possibly not,' said the woman, staring into space for several seconds.

The DI paused, slightly puzzled but quickly moved on.

'All right, did you threaten revenge upon Miss Glass whilst at the school or at any other time?'

'No.'

'So, when did you think about causing her trouble?'

'Not until Miss Sweet's remains were found. That's when I got the idea and decided to come to the police station.'

'Did you ever have any doubts about what you were doing?'

'Yes, often.'

'So, why did you not come forward and own up to what you had done, particularly once the trial had started? Miss Glass might have hanged for a murder she didn't commit if she had not taken her own life.'

'I would never have let her hang, despite her dreadful reputation and my feelings toward her.'

'Easy to say now, Miss Austen, but only you know whether or not that is really true. You could have done the decent thing and come forward even after Miss Glass had committed suicide but you didn't. Why not?'

'I don't really know, I suppose because I was frightened of the consequences.'

'But you must have realised that, sooner or later, the truth would probably come out.'

'Yes, I suppose I did. I don't know, I didn't think things through. I imagine, I assumed, she would be found not guilty and that no one would know the truth.'

'Well, Miss Austen I think you're going to have an awful long time to think things through as you put it.

'Anyway, regarding your statement, it seems from our investigations that your story was a mixture of fact and fiction in that when you said that you had seen two men that has been confirmed by our enquiries. So, have you any idea when Miss Sweet was actually killed that evening?

'No, I don't, Mr Carlsen, I didn't hear anything much, just the thunder. I must have walked right passed her body, or at least where it ended up, how awful.

'What about the hut, did you hear any noise coming from it on your way home?'

'No.'

'And do you know personally who killed Miss Sweet?'

'No.'

'And did you, at any time, see or hear your former headmistress or Miss Glass during your visit to the quarry that evening?'

'No.'

'How long were you in your hidey hole?'

'About forty minutes.'

'When did you arrive and what time did you leave the quarry?'

'I suppose I arrived about eight o'clock and left at about eight forty-five.'

'So, having seen the men when you walked along the path, it's only regarding subsequent events that that you decided to tell lies, why did you choose that course of action?'

'Well, I suppose I thought that it might sound more credible, especially given the passage of time; I guessed that you'd probably trace the men, which indeed you did and that would at least, in part, confirm my version of events. I had no idea that they would become involved in murder.'

'Instead, you wasted OUR valuable time following a lead which resulted in a false accusation against Miss Glass and probably her untimely death.'

'Yes, I'm so, so sorry,' she said as tears started to roll slowly down her cheeks.

'Are you prepared to give us a statement under caution detailing exactly what happened?'

'Yes, anything you like.'

'Well, it'd better be the truth this time.'

'Yes, I promise.'

'All right, Miss Austen,' announced the chief inspector later, after the statement had been taken, 'Once we have consulted with our solicitors, you will be charged with perjury based on the evidence you gave at Worcester Assizes in the trial of Leticia Glass and also with giving a false statement to police. And when you appear at Malvern magistrates court, we will be opposing bail unless someone guarantees a sum of money that you will not abscond.'

Austen nodded, dabbing her cheek with a handkerchief.

'I think that about does it, John,' said Martin later, 'I think she'll plead and that will be that. But I do wonder when exactly Sweet was killed that evening, ironically it could have been while Austin was there.'

'We'll probably never know, sir, certainly Austen looked remorseful enough,' said Carlsen.

'Yep, so she damn well ought. I'll get onto Fowler and let him know. It's a hell of a thing to do, even to somebody like Leticia Glass. You know it still gripes with me that we were fooled by Austen, and the consequences of it all.'

'Well, I feel the same, sir, but as I've said before, it was nobody's fault, it's all part of the horrible job we do. Anyway, I'll arrange a press conference, no doubt more silly questions.'

Later, DCI Martin again found himself in Fowler's office. The detective superintendent stared at him for a few seconds, hands folded across the edge of his desk.

'A bit of a mess, eh, Mr Martin?' he remarked after a long pause, his long fingers tapping against each other.

'I'm afraid so, yes, sir,' said the DCI, waiting for the bomb to drop.

'Well, no blame can be placed at your door. You have the chief constable's support and you have mine. You couldn't possibly have foreseen the turn of events, our legal people didn't either. If it hadn't been for that pansy putting his hands up, we'd never have guessed anyway and especially if that gardener had not found the wallet in the first place. But it's all a little late for the Glass woman.

'And there's still the Adams murder to sort out,' continued Fowler, 'so next steps, Mr Martin?'

'I plan to review the evidence, sir, and get Worcester to double-check the prints, which were all over the place at the scene in case we might have missed something. Other than that, we need a breakthrough of some sort.'

The interview ended as amicably as it had begun, and after returning to the office, Martin called a conference with DI Carlsen and DS Roberts.

'Well, Mr Fowler is looking for progress on the Adams affair. If we don't have a lucky break soon, I can see the chief constable calling in the Yard which will be the ultimate insult.'

Three months later, Celia Austen pleaded guilty to perjury at Worcester Assizes and was sentenced to six years' imprisonment. Two weeks after her arrival at Holloway prison, she was found dead in her cell. She had hanged herself. There was no note.

Some weeks later Jesse Thurrock also appeared at Worcester Assizes and pleaded not guilty to the murders of John Perks and Dorothy Sweet but was eventually convicted of the murder of the railwayman and the manslaughter of the headmistress.

The appeal court upheld his conviction and his plea for clemency to the Home Secretary also failed. Accordingly, one foggy evening before Christmas, a man carrying a heavy brief case knocked on the gate of Oxford gaol and was taken to the condemned cell where Jesse Thurrock awaited his fate. The man took measurements and then, after examining the execution shed, left for his lodgings in the town. Early the following morning, he returned, and at precisely 9 a.m. in the presence of the prison governor and chaplain, Thurrock, having declined to say anything, had his head covered and was taken quickly to the adjacent execution shed where his legs were shackled and he was guided to the chalk markings on the door under his feet; he didn't struggle. The executioner pulled a lever and Thurrock plunged into the drop breaking his neck.

Outside, a small crowd, which had gathered as they always did for such an event, slowly melted away but not before a man emerged briefly through a wicket in the main gates of the prison and removed the Notice of Execution which had been pinned up the previous day. Among the group was Edna Perks and the former Mrs Thurrock but neither was aware of the other.

And on the opposite side of the street, a woman shouted 'ghouls' several times before she was persuaded by a policeman to go on her way.

And Edna Perks wept before slowly walking away into the mist.

Diana Davies observed the scene some distance away but kept her thoughts to herself.

Back at Malvern police station, DI Carlsen looked at his watch.

'Well, that's that, sir, Thurrock should be well on his way to the next world by now.'

'They're welcome to him,' said Martin, 'a nasty bit of work, but I suppose we have to give the man credit for admitting to Sweet's death, otherwise we'd be thrashing about in the dark and her family would still know nothing. But at least they can now enjoy some peace. And so can Edna Perks.

'Anyway, about those breakings up at Belle Vue.'

Chapter 22

'The results of the review of the fingerprints in the Adams case have arrived, John,' called out the detective chief inspector one day the following week, 'they've listed those that were found and compared them to the names of the people that attended the scene.'

'Any surprises, sir? Carlsen asked.

'Well, yes actually, come in and close the door. Do we know if DC Empson was ever there?'

The DI shook his head and looked puzzled.

'No, he was on leave that day, because I remember thinking we could have done with his help. Anyhow, he shouldn't have been on the list we submitted to Worcester, sir, why do you ask?'

'Well, what's strange is the fact that his dabs have turned up at the scene on the frame of the back door where the attacker gained entrance, but they're partial and not blood stained,' said Martin. 'As you say, his name wasn't on our list we initially sent to Worcester so they must have checked all our CID against their records second time around by accident.'

'Oh dear,' commented Carlsen.

'Yes, oh dear, but I could think of a stronger word.'

The two men exchanged nervous glances.

'There is, of course, one obvious possibility that neither of us wants to consider,' said Martin, 'but we'd better have another look at the crime books, CID diaries and station messages and see whether CID, and especially Empson ever went up there before Adams was murdered. We'll keep it to ourselves for the moment, there might be a perfectly innocent explanation, especially as there's no blood on the prints. Or it might be that he left his dabs on the way in before the encounter with the woman which, given that the murderer possessed thin gloves for the actual killing, could be considered careless. Equally, the prints could have been left on some other occasion.'

'Yes, sir, I suppose we have to hope that there is an innocent explanation. We can always ask him whether he's ever been near the place without giving the impression we're casting aspersions.'

DI Carlsen spent that evening looking through CID and station records and was on the point of giving up when he found a message relating to a man being seen acting suspiciously in Graham Road near Adams's house about seven months prior to the murder. CID officers attended but there were no names.

'I've found a reference to CID and uniform attending a suspect call near Adams's house a while ago, sir,' reported Carlsen to Martin the following morning, 'but there's no mention of anyone by name.'

'Well, I think we'd better bite the bullet and ask him,' replied Martin, 'we can always wrap it up by saying that we need to clarify who was up there that day but without necessarily implying that he might be a suspect or that his prints have been found.'

'DC Empson, in my office, please,' called the DCI.

'Empson, we're reviewing the evidence in the Adams's enquiry and we've come across a message received at the nick a month or two prior to her murder relating to a suspect seen acting suspiciously up in Graham Road not far from her house. We want to know who went up there that evening because nothing's on the messages. Did you attend?'

'I think I did, sir, yes. Seem to recall we knocked on the doors of a few houses to make sure there'd been no breakings. That probably included Olive Adams but I don't remember. I do remember that nobody was ever nicked and that was that.'

'All right, Empson, can you remember who else went up there?'

'DC Richards, oh, and I think, DS Roberts and a couple of uniform.'

'Yes, all right, we'll talk to them. Thanks.'

'Well, sir,' commented Carlsen, 'he's either being entirely straight with us or he realises what we're at and is covering his back for just this eventuality; he's a bright lad and we shouldn't underestimate him. I suppose from his point of view, it's a good thing that there was that incident with the suspect ahead of the murder, it gives him a possible way out. All I can say is, I hope to God he's not involved but I've got this terrible feeling.'

The DI shivered involuntarily.

'Yeah, so have I,' replied the DCI. 'I don't like conducting this subterfuge against one of our own, I really don't, but there we are. Anyway, I'd better mention it to Mr Fowler.

'John, I'm off to see the guvnor again,' said Martin later, 'I seem to spend more time in his office than mine these days; I imagine it's about Empson.'

'I'm sorry to call you over here again so soon, Mr Martin,' Fowler was saying, closing his office door, 'but something else has come up on DC Empson which you ought to know about, I didn't want to talk about it on the phone.'

The DCI's heart sank.

'We've come across something in a crime book which suggests that Empson has had dealings with Olive Adams before. This was several years back when he was at Bromsgrove as a new DC. She apparently had a breaking at her then address and Empson was the officer in the case. It seems that something happened and it ended up in a complaint against him. It was eventually squared up and nothing resulted but you need to be aware of it. It was just luck that a DI over there was looking for something else and came across the record. The Adams murder rang a bell and his guvnor contacted me.'

'What was the complaint all about, sir, do we know?'

'No, unfortunately, but you know what it's like, unless it's really serious, nobody is willing to commit pen to paper just in case the wheel comes off and they have to answer for what they've written. There was nothing criminal, as far as I know, probably more disciplinary than anything else and that was that. So just keep a watching brief and we'll review the situation from time to time.

'Your information on Empson's prints being found at the house is not good news, Mr Martin, but it's not necessarily evidence of Empson's involvement. Nothing further needs doing as regards him at the moment so, as I said before, just keep an eye on him, unless you come up with some hard evidence.

'Oh, I should just warn you that the chief constable was muttering about calling in the Yard if we don't make some progress on Adams soon. Now, we don't want that, do we?'

DCI Martin returned to his office in subdued mood and explained the situation to John Carlsen.

'The guvnor just wants a watching brief, John, but it's very worrying. I don't like the idea that one of our blokes might be bent. That aside, I want the lads to chase up their informants see if there's anything they can tell us regarding the Adams killing. I know we did it at the time, but we've got to do something and somebody may have heard a more recent whisper especially if we wave a few bob in front of their noses. We can't lose anything by it.

'And you should also know we're certainly being threatened with a visit from the Yard.'

'Oh dear, all right, sir, message received.'

Chapter 23

The following morning, alone in his office, Detective Chief Inspector Martin consumed frequent cups of tea and wondered how to proceed with the Adams investigation. He wracked his brains for inspiration and constantly fiddled with a piece of paper and pencil, as if wishing for the solution to suddenly appear on the blank sheet. After all, nothing so nasty like as this had occurred in Malvern before to his knowledge and they were rare elsewhere in his experience. He had completed a review of the case so far and stared at the case papers in front of him, the possible link with Empson being a constant worry. He wished there was an alternative suspect, but every time he applied his mind to the matter, the figure of DC Empson loomed in his thinking and he just couldn't shake it off. It all reminded him of an incident as a young detective when a colleague with whom he was working arrested a man on flimsy evidence. It soon became clear that his colleague was going to tell lies to the court and that he, Martin, was expected to back a new version of events in his own evidence. Ultimately, the suspect pleaded guilty, and he didn't have to stand in the witness box. He had often wondered since whether he could have gone through with it. Thinking about it, he was very much afraid that he would have done. And then what? It would have made him as guilty as, say, Celia Austen. But that was then. What was he going to do now with an unsolved murder on his hands? And one of his own detectives the possible culprit.

He was no further forward when, suddenly, there was a commotion coming from downstairs.

'What's going on, Sergeant White?' Martin called from the top of the stairs.

'Somebody with a knife tried to do in an old man at 14, Como Road, sir, place called Holdfast House, apparently he's still alive but it could be touch and go; uniform are chasing a suspect.'

'All right, I'll get up there. Empson, where's Empson?' he bellowed from his office.

'He's on leave until next week, sir,' replied DC Jones.

'Right, grab the spare car and take me up to the address.'

The two raced up to Como Road to be met by an out-of-breath uniformed constable.

'What's happening?' the chief inspector asked, the police car skidding to a halt.

'The gardener at number 14 called for help after he found the owner with a stab wound. An ambulance has just taken the man to hospital and he's in a bad way.'

'What about the suspect?'

'We've lost him, sir, but he must be close by somewhere.'

'Description?'

'None but probably blood on him.'

'All right, get back to the address and stay there with the gardener until we return.'

Martin reached for the microphone of the car radio and spoke to County control room.

'This is DCI Martin, Malvern, I have a suspect for a wounding on the loose in Como Road, no description but may be carrying a knife and will probably have blood stains on him. I want as many officers as you can spare, I don't care where you get them from, but direct them to number 14, Como Road, called Holdfast House, and I or one of my officers will meet them there. Also see if you can contact DI Carlsen, he should be out in a Malvern CID car somewhere, save me doing it. Finally, I want another ambulance on standby up here.'

Martin had just finished speaking when DS Roberts appeared.

'Where did you spring from, what's the latest?'

'Well, I was dealing with a burglary just along the road and was just finishing and heard some shouting. You've heard about an injured man, sir, I suppose? He's gone to Worcester Infirmary. The suspect we think is somewhere close by, he was chased by a passing PC but has gone to ground.'

'All right, I've called for help from County, we'll go up to the scene and await for assistance. Is there any description, because I haven't been given one yet?'

'No, sir, the PC who was chasing him didn't get a very good look at him, the victim's gardener may be able to help though.'

'All right, check the house and gardens of, say, numbers 10, 12 and 16 Como and then come up to number 14.'

'Right, sir.'

A moment or two later, the police car drew up outside the address.

'I'm Detective Chief Inspector Martin, Malvern police,' he announced to a man who was standing by a side gate.

'I'm Newnes, the gardener, somebody tried to kill Mr Carden, it's terrible, how could anyone do such a thing?'

'Can you describe the suspect?' asked Martin.

'About five foot ten, I suppose, quite big, going bald; that's about it really.'

'How old do you think?'

'Mid to late- thirties.'

'Right, get on the radio,' said Martin to the DC, 'put out that description and tell 'em the suspect may have blood stains on him. And reinforce the fact that he may be carrying a knife. Also, ask about the assistance they're supposed to be sending us. And I want an officer at the Infirmary with the victim just in case the worst happens.'

Jones returned within a couple of minutes.

'I've done that, sir, Worcester are sending five constables and a couple of DCs. DI Carlsen is also on his way as is Detective Superintendent Fowler. And somebody from Worcester will go to the Infirmary.'

'Good, now tell me what happened, Mr Newnes? said Martin, addressing the gardener, 'take your time.'

'Well, I was working in the kitchen garden at the back, like, when I heard this shout. I ran around the front and found Mr Carden lying in the hallway with the front door open. There was blood everywhere and I saw a man run into the road.'

Suddenly, a constable hurried in from the road.

'Sir, somebody has told me that there's some shouting coming from number 22 Como, one of the others has gone up there to have a look.'

'All right, I'll go up there, Jones, you stay here with Mr Newnes and see if he can help us any further; tell anyone who arrives where we are.'

A few doors along, people were stopping and staring outside number 22, but on arrival nothing could be heard from inside the house.

'Right, when I've asked one or two basic questions, get these people away from here, minimum a hundred yards both sides,' Martin instructed two local constables who had just appeared, 'and watch out, the press will probably soon appear and they get up to all sorts of tricks. Don't let them do anything without my authority.'

'Who's inside the house, can anybody help?' Martin then enquired after introducing himself to a small crowd of bystanders.

'Well, I saw a man rush into the drive a few minutes ago,' replied one 'there was a shout and I've heard nothing since. I think he must have panicked because he suddenly swerved off the road as if he didn't really know where he was going.'

'Yes, that's right,' murmured a woman who was standing next to him, 'nasty looking piece of work.'

'From what direction did the man come?' said the chief inspector.

'The same way as you've just have. He was out of breath and limping a bit.

'OK, what did he look like?'

'Oh, tallish, quite a big man and a bit thin on top, about late thirties, I suppose,' the woman replied.

'All right, who lives here, does anybody know?'

People shook their heads.

'All right, thanks, please move up the road, it'll be safer and all of you give your names and addresses to the constables, please. We may need to speak to you in more detail later.'

Malvern CID car pulled up and DI Carlsen emerged to be met by the DCI.

'How much of the story do you know so far, John?'

'I've heard about the stabbing and one of our PCs says something is going on here as well.

'Does it sound like Empson, sir?' he then asked quietly.

'I don't know, but the description given by the gardener and one of the crowd could match and that's a worry.'

DS Roberts hurried up the road and joined them.

'No luck at those addresses adjacent to number 14, sir, I presume he's gone to ground, has he?'

'Could be, sarge,' replied Carlsen, 'someone heard a shout. See if you can find out who lives here and what access there might be at the back. We might need to get in there in a hurry. And check out the garden, the suspect might get out that way. If possible, we need to check the house adjoining the back as well. I've already got a PC at the rear of the place but take another one with you, he can help with the search if you can get over the fence.'

'I think the cavalry, including Fowler, will be arriving from Worcester soon, John,' continued Martin, 'so we'd better have a plan once Roberts has done his recce. There's only been one shout from somebody in the house right at the start and nothing since; don't know who it was.'

A few minutes later, Roberts returned with a PC.

'Someone called Bronstein lives at the address, sir, an elderly man, apparently keeps himself to himself and is not often seen. There is one other access door at the back, looks as if hasn't been used in years and the walls are covered in ivy right up to the second floor. The garden has a tall, evergreen hedge surrounding it, so I think our suspect will have a problem getting out that way.'

'All right, John,' said Martin, 'I'll take a PC with me and bang on the door, see if I can get a response. Come with me, constable.'

The two men walked up the short drive and the DCI banged loudly on the door.

'This Detective Chief Inspector Martin of Malvern police,' he called through the brass letterbox, 'can anybody hear me?'

There was no reply, so Martin repeated the question. There was still no answer and he returned to the road just as a car and van with officers from Worcester arrived.

'Right, what's happening, Mr Martin?' Detective Superintendent Fowler asked, levering his bulk out of the car with some difficulty.

The detective chief inspector explained.

'Do we know whether it's Empson?' Fowler asked, lowering his voice to a whisper.

'No, sir, there's only been a single shout from the property and that was before we arrived. I've banged on the door but got no response, and no one has shown themselves at any of the front windows of the house. There are two separate descriptions of a suspect, which could be Empson but can't be sure; anyway, it's gone out on the radio.'

Fowler nodded and then thought for a moment.

'All right, we're going to have to break in. As a precaution, I've brought a couple of armed officers with me. One can go inside with me, the other can stay outside in case chummy tries to make a run for it. We're assuming he's still in there and, of course, there's the knife to consider. What do you reckon is the best way in?'

'Well, there is a back door, sir, DS Roberts has checked it out. Apparently, the back wall is smothered in ivy, might be able to use that especially if one of the upper windows is open.'

'Yeah, but that might be a bit of a last resort, Mr Martin, you stay with me for the moment. Mr Carlsen, take a look and try to force the rear door, use one of my armed DCs to watch your back. Give me a shout when you think you're in and I'll come around, or through the front if you can open the door. Oh, and take this,' said Fowler, handing Carlsen a jemmy.

The inspector and the detective constable walked around the back of the house and carefully examined the solid back door which was locked and also covered in ivy. It had clearly not been opened in a long time.

'Think you can manage it, sir?' DC Baker asked, hand on the pistol which hung heavily in his left-hand jacket pocket.'

'There's only one way to find out,' replied Carlsen as he tried to lever the door open with the jemmy. But despite much effort and considerable splintering the door refused to budge.

The DI cursed.

'I could try shooting the lock off, sir,' suggested the DC helpfully.

'No, you're not Hopalong Cassidy, we've got to think of something else.'

Carlsen's gaze ranged over the upper windows.

'There's a window open on the second floor if we can get at it, but it's going to be mighty tricky, the only way is up the ivy and Mr Fowler won't like that idea, but go and tell him anyway.'

After a while, Fowler and Martin appeared around the corner and they discussed the situation.

'No, no point in any of us breaking our necks, Mr Carlsen, we'll get in here by breaking one of the ground floor windows and the frame if necessary. I'll go in when DC James here has done the jemmying and, if possible, open the front door. A couple of you can then come in the house and we can search the place.'

'I can do it, sir, if you like,' suggested Martin.

'No, it's about time I got my hands dirty again, and besides I'm paid more than you. You can lead the search with Mr Carlsen once we're in. Come on, DC James, got that jemmy? We'll try the door again, then the window, you take my torch. Keep my other armed man out the front, Mr Martin. All right, let's get on with it.'

The DC then tried again to force the jemmy between the door and the frame but he was soon sweating and the door still refused to budge.

'Right, never mind, leave the door and try one of these windows,' instructed Fowler.

This proved rather easier and the window frame soon gave way under the onslaught with fragments of glass and old putty tumbling onto the windowsill and flowerbed below.

'I'll go first, son,' said Fowler, 'I'll take the jemmy but you have the pistol and keep your head down; above all, don't shoot me up the arse.'

The detective superintendent struggled to get through the window, and although not a slim man, he at last succeeded but breathing heavily. But even from the inside, the back door still would not open and the place was in semi-darkness.

'We'll do the ground floor first,' said Fowler, 'stay right behind me and see if you can find a light switch. We need to get to the front door.'

The torch that was being held by James suddenly went out and the two men became separated. Fowler collided with the staircase in the dark and then heard a noise from ahead of him and could just discern a figure coming down.

'Watch out!' called Fowler as the young detective struggled to get the torch to work.

From James, there was no answer but, suddenly, Fowler was suddenly aware of a hand high up in the air holding a cosh which then crashed down on to the front of his head before falling on the floor with a clatter. The detective stumbled back and fell to the floor in a shower of lights that flashed before his eyes. He tried to struggle to his feet and was aware of somebody picking up the pistol which had been dropped by James in the scrimmage at the bottom of the stairs. He looked through a semi-conscious haze and in the gloom became aware of a man pointing the gun straight at him.

'Don't, don't be a bloody fool,' Fowler said, having difficulty with his words whilst gripping on to the bannister and struggling to his feet, 'put the gun down.'

Suddenly, there was a click as the hammer on the weapon was pulled back, followed by a flash and a bang. Fowler fell back to the floor, blood pouring down the side of his face and lay there moaning.

'Urgent assistance, please,' shouted DC James as the others started to force their way in through the broken window and the front door.

After several moments of confusion, somebody found a light switch.

'Oh, God it's the guvnor,' said Martin, as Fowler lay on the floor at the bottom of the stairs, bleeding heavily from a head wound. 'Get the ambulance men in here, Roberts, it looks as if the suspect got hold of James's gun, then put out a message that there is an armed suspect on the loose of the same description that we gave before. If Mr Fowler dies, I'll hang the bastard myself, and especially if it's our mutual friend.'

Martin took off his coat and placed it gently under the man's head.

Meanwhile, DC James stood in silence, head cupped in both hands.

'Not your fault, lad, you couldn't have anticipated what was going to happen. Go outside and get some air, we'll talk later,' said Carlsen.

'Right, the rest of us will start searching the house floor by floor,' instructed Martin. 'I'll lead the way. Knox, give me your pistol. And don't forget, the suspect could still be in here with one of our guns, and look out for the owner of the house, he could be hurt. Constable Matthews, stay here with Mr Fowler and go with him in the ambulance; it'll probably be the Infirmary, wait there with him. The front door is open so they can probably get him out that way and ring Malvern nick when you have some news of Mr Fowler's condition.'

The ground floor was searched, but of the suspect and the owner, there was no trace. Then Martin started to mount the stairs which were still in partial darkness. Suddenly, a figure vaulted over the bannisters from above them and tore out of the house through the front door, dropping the gun as he went. He reached the road and bowled over a uniformed officer who tried to grab him.

'Stop him,' shouted the constable, more in hope than expectation as he picked himself up. The man then ran up the road, limping as he went but fell over in a tangle with a detective, who having heard a shout was hurrying around the corner.

'I don't know what you've done, mate, but you're nicked,' said the officer breathlessly as he tried to handcuff the large man who was struggling on the ground. A PC rushed to help.

'Right, search him and then you can help me get him into the van,' the detective instructed the constable. 'What exactly has he done?'

'He shot Mr Fowler; he's been injured in the head. There's also been a stabbing, so we need to look for a knife; we've already got the gun and a cosh. Ah, there it is,' said the PC as a blood-smeared blade fell out of a pocket onto the pavement.

'So, you shot my guvnor, did you?' the detective said to the man who was now lying handcuffed on the ground.

'Well,' he said, as the two bundled him into the police van, 'don't expect any favours, God help you if he dies. Mate, ' he instructed the PC, 'go and tell 'em that we've got a body and then we'll take him to the nick.'

The PC hurried inside and almost bumped into DI Carlsen who was coming out of the front door.

'The suspect has been arrested, sir.'

'Thank God for that,' replied the DI just as the ambulance crew struggled to get the stretcher through the front door. But soon Fowler was placed gently in the ambulance and driven away accompanied by the constable.

'Where's the arresting officer?' the DI asked.

'In the van, sir, with the prisoner.'

'Good, who nicked him?'

'I think it's DC Empson, sir.'

'EMPSON? Are you sure?'

'What's the matter, sir? You look like you've seen a ghost.'

'I, um,' stuttered Carlsen, 'what's Empson doing here?'

'I was coming up the road and he banged into me, bit of luck, eh?' the detective answered from inside the van.

'But I thought you were on leave.'

'Well, I am, sir, but I happened to pop in the nick for something and heard this was going on so I thought I'd come up and help.'

'Well, I'm glad you did,' replied the detective inspector, hardly believing his ears, 'otherwise we might still be running around Malvern looking for him. What's his name?'

'Clover, sir, Billy Clover, we've met before.'

Meanwhile in the house, the search continued for the owner and officers were just on the point of giving up when a wardrobe door in the main bedroom swung slowly open.

'I'm Doctor Bernstein,' said a querulous voice from the gloom, 'a man forced me into the cupboard and told me to stay here or he'd kill me. Are you the police? Has he gone yet?'

'Yes, we're the police, you're quite safe now, sir, he's been arrested,' replied Martin.'

The elderly man was then helped to a chair.

'Are you all right, sir?'

'Yes, just a little shaken, I need to sit down.'

'Have you any family we can contact for you?' the DCI asked.

'I've got a son; I can telephone him but I'll be all right.'

'I presume you let the man in, Doctor Bernstein?'

'Yes, when I heard knocking at the front door, I thought it was a friend of mine visiting. But a young man attacked me, I couldn't stop him from coming in, he said he had a knife; I shouted but it was no good.'

Carlsen joined the group in the bedroom.

'Could I have a quiet word, sir, please? The suspect's been nicked.'

'Our man, I suppose?' said Martin quietly.

'No, sir, you're not going to believe this but Empson is the arresting officer.'

'But it can't be there must be some mistake.'

'No mistake, sir, the suspect banged into Empson who happened to be coming up the road. The man is somebody called Billy Clover, don't know anything about him yet but his name rings a bell; he's on his way to the nick.'

'But it just doesn't make sense, John. I was so certain; this business must have shrivelled my brain. Anyway, the main concern now is how Mr Fowler is; get on the wireless and ask Worcester to check his condition with the Infirmary rather than wait for our PC to phone in. Get photographs etc. organised, oh, and ask County to inform the chief constable.'

'Will be done, sir,' replied Carslen, who hurried to the car.

The following morning early, the chief constable arrived at Malvern and convened a conference in the DCI's office.

'Firstly, I've been to the Infirmary, gentlemen, and I'm pleased to report that Mr Fowler is out of danger. The wound, although a nasty one, is not a threat to his life. The bullet missed entering his skull by a fraction apparently, just causing a nasty scrape on the scalp. How the hell the suspect missed killing him from that short range, heaven knows; Mr Fowler's a lucky man.

'Everybody did a good job yesterday, for which thank you,' he continued. 'I gather the owner of number 14, Carden, is not as badly hurt as at first thought?'

'That's right, sir, but nevertheless he's still seriously injured but the hospital think he's got a good chance of pulling through.'

'And the man at number 22?'

'Doctor Bernstein? He's all right, more shaken up than anything else. But he is getting on a bit so it will take a while for him to recover but he's staying with a relative.'

'A surprise though is your DC Empson, I assumed the worst as I think you did?'

'Well, it's a relief, sir, believe you me,' said Martin, 'in fact, we've a lot to thank Empson for otherwise we might still be chasing our tails.'

'I had a brief chat with Mr Fowler before I was chased away by the nurses and he's convinced that he was shot by Empson, it must have been the crack on the head he got before the shooting. So, what do we know about the suspect Clover?'

'Well, strangely enough, sir, he was involved, in a manner of speaking, with the Sweet murder all those years ago,' continued DCI Martin. 'When she disappeared, he was working as a groundsman at the college and somebody thought he might have been involved but there was never any evidence. Basically, he's a drunk with several previous for malicious damage, mostly at local pubs and he's got a violent temper. I would have thought this latest stuff was not in his league as he's a bit dim but he said that he knocked on the door of number 14 Como Road asking for gardening work but that the owner told him to go away in no uncertain terms, at which he took umbrage and forced his way in. When the owner tried to stop him, Clover stabbed the man then panicked and ran to number 22. There's no reason to doubt that's the way things went. And we've got our gun back, plus the cosh he belted Mr Fowler with and the knife he used on Carden which was found on our suspect.'

'The knife makes it the same M.O. for the Adams murder, doesn't it?' asked the chief constable.

'Well, certainly the use of a knife does fit but we haven't talked to him about that yet, sir, although he wasn't wearing gloves in this latest lot of offences as we suspect that the Adams murderer was. Anyhow, Clover's still in the frame for it, I can't imagine he's going to deny it. The only thing is that his prints weren't found at the scene of the Adams murder, but there was a lot of mess there and many smudged dabs so it's possible that they're there somewhere but that won't help in nailing him. Of course, he doesn't need to know that, so we can hit him with that one as appropriate. To date, we've charged him with attempted murder on Mr Fowler and Carden, plus grievous bodily harm on both and then

177

hopefully with the Adams killing as well in due course. If necessary, we can get him to a special sitting of the magistrates court this afternoon.

'One thing we are both relieved about, sir, is that this Empson business has been cleared up. I had visions of him sitting on the charge room bench, especially as the description given by witnesses could have fitted.'

'I couldn't agree more, Mr Martin, something less for us all to worry about. A crooked officer is the last thing we want; I regret we suspected him in the first place. Well, I'll let you get on, gentlemen, keep me up to date via my clerk and I'll keep an eye on Mr Fowler; knowing him, he'll try and discharge himself from hospital too early. Oh, by the way, has a press conference been organised yet? I noticed the usual scrum at the front of the station when I came in.'

'Yes, sir, later this morning.'

'All right, carry on and well done.'

'That's a turn up, sir,' commented Carlsen, after the chief constable had left, 'fancy him darkening the doors of Malvern nick, probably hasn't happened since I was a babe in arms.'

'Umph,' grunted Martin, 'I'd lay a bet that if it had been one of our DCs who'd been shot, he probably wouldn't have bothered but there's the officer class for you. By the way, I've had a word with DC James's guvnor over at Worcester, apparently the lad thinks he was responsible for the attack on Mr Fowler. Feels very bad about it and thinks he might be sent back to uniform in disgrace or, worse, sacked. But he's been told that it was not his fault and that he's got nothing to reproach himself about, which is quite right. Hopefully, Fowler can reassure him on that.

'Anyway, back to work, we need to talk to this idiot Clover about Olive Adams so we can charge him with the lot as soon as possible; it'll save a lot of messing about. We'll chat to him when his solicitor gets back, he's due back here in about twenty minutes. We can all go down the pub once he's been to court.'

'I must say he doesn't much fit the description given to us by that so-called witness in the Adams's business. He was described as "official looking", that's not something I'd call Clover,' said Carlsen.'

'Oh, I dunno, he's quite smart for a gardener, in dress if not in head. In any case, it could be two separate people plus the witness was elderly and some way off. I don't think we need worry too much, you know how unreliable some people can be, like Austen in a different sense.'

'Don't remind me of that woman, sir,' commented Carlsen bitterly, 'it makes me seethe.'

'Yes, well, I'll try not to but she's constantly in the back of my mind.'

Early that afternoon after the press conference had finished, Martin and Carlsen were approached by Diana Davies.

'Well done to you both,' she said, 'I'll make sure that we say something nice about you in the Gazette. But you also said that investigations into the Adams murder were continuing, so is Clover likely to be charged?'

'I certainly hope so, but only time will tell, Miss Davies,' replied DCI Martin. 'I assure you, as ever, you'll be the first to know.'

The journalist nodded and left.

'You know, John, I think she's the only journalist I could ever get close to trusting,' commented Martin, 'pretty too.'

'Right, time for a cuppa and then we must get on,' he continued, 'trouble is, we still haven't had confirmation from Worcester that his knife was also used on Olive Adams, but I can't think that's going to be a problem. We'll get him charged as soon as possible and then get on the blower to the magistrates' clerk.'

Fifteen minutes later, Martin and Carlsen, together with Jenks, Clover's solicitor, entered the interview room and sat down opposite the prisoner.

'Right, Mr Clover,' said DI Carlsen, 'you are still under caution and we now want to move on from the attempted murder of Mr Carden and Detective Superintendent Fowler and question you regarding the death of Olive Adams on 27 October 1937; what can you tell us about that?'

'Olive who?' replied Clover.

'Olive Adams,' repeated Martin, 'at number 10, Graham Road, a place called "The Camelias".'

'Don't know nothing about her,' said Clover.

'I hope this is not going to be a difficult interview, Clover, you've already admitted to offences committed involving Mr Carden and Mr Fowler and you have been charged with those. We need you to cooperate so we can clear the Olive Adams business up as well; there's no point in denying your involvement.'

'Yeah, I know, just to clear the books, I think you blokes say, don't yer? Well, I'm not co-operating, like, and in any case, your detective Empson threatened me.'

'Look,' said Carlsen, 'we know you're responsible, you used the same M.O. on that old woman as you did up at Como Road.'

'M what?' Clover replied, looking puzzled.

'Modus Operandi, the way a criminal usually behaves at the scene of a crime and in your case the knife.'

'Well, I didn't commit no crime there. I know I stabbed that old man, but I never did that woman and I'm not going to go down for nothing I didn't do; you're not hanging me.'

'Look, it's not just the knife, there were fingerprints everywhere at the house and we've got yours on record, it's only a matter of time before we get a match. You've done quite a bit over the years, smashing up pubs and generally making a nuisance of yourself.'

'Yeah, I know I've been in trouble and I'm a bit stupid, like, but I've never murdered nobody.'

'Oh, but you might have if that old man in Como Road dies, or our guvnor come to that. You're quite happy to go around stabbing and shooting people or hitting them over the head just because you feel like it, and that's what happened to that poor old lady and you were responsible for her death, weren't you?'

'No, I wasn't and you won't find my fingerprints, like, because I wasn't there, you're trying to bullshit me. Anyway, I haven't been well, like, that's why I do these things.'

'Including Olive Adams?' suggested Carlsen.

'No, I told you I didn't do it. How many more times?'

'Look, Mr Clover, you almost killed two men yesterday, we've every reason to believe that you killed Miss Adams because she refused or was unable to offer you gardening work just like Mr Carden and you lost your temper and stabbed her and then smashed her over the head. That's right, isn't it?'

'No, I'm telling you I didn't kill her.'

'I think we're going around in circles, Mr Carlsen,' interrupted the solicitor. 'I don't think there is anything further to be gained by pursuing this line of questioning.'

'All right, we'll stop for the present,' acknowledged the DI.

'I must be losing my touch, sir,' said Carlsen outside, 'I'd stake my pension on Clover being responsible for that murder.'

'Yeah, it's a puzzle, John, trouble is, I'm not quite sure where we go from here, we've got no evidence placing him at the scene. His dabs could have been amongst that mess but he didn't fall for it when we mentioned the possibility that they were.'

'No, maybe he's not as stupid as we take him for. If the boys at County say that the knife was used in both instances, and I've a feeling they may not, we're back on safe ground. If they don't, we're sunk, and it won't do the chief constable's ulcers any good either. Trouble is that the one witness we've got didn't get a very good look at him, so an identification parade is a waste of time. Do you know, I can't believe that there is someone else roaming around our patch sticking knives in people? It just doesn't make sense.'

There was a tap on the office door. It was Jenks, the solicitor.

'I've had another word with my client, he's adamant that he was not involved in the murder of Olive Adams but he wishes to talk about some burglaries in the Pickersleigh Road area.'

'Oh, does he?' replied Martin, 'well, at least that's progress, but I hope he's not trying to do a deal with us, Mr Jenks.'

'No, he realises that you might think that.'

The two detectives were about to return to the interview room when the phone rang in Martin's office. Carlsen answered it.

'It's Worcester, sir, that knife from yesterday's business in Como Road, it's a different weapon from the one used on Miss Adams, different shape blade.'

'Well, that's it, John,' said the DCI, looking crestfallen, 'we've lost it, where to now?'

Clover was eventually committed for trial to Worcester Assizes in relation to Carden and Fowler but nothing could connect him to the murder of Olive Adams. He was convicted of two offences of attempted murder and five burglaries and was sentenced to life imprisonment with penal servitude.

'Well, at least we got him for Fowler and Carden, if not for poor Olive,' commented Martin after sentence had been passed, 'but unfortunately the months keep rolling by and we're still no further forward.'

Chapter 24

A few days later, DCI Martin was sitting in his office, thumbing through a pile of papers when Sergeant Hughes knocked on his door.

'There's a man downstairs, sir, says that he has some important information on the Adams murder, he's pretty insistent, a fellow called Collins.'

'All right, I'll get Mr Carlsen to have a chat.'

'John, do that will you?' Martin called.

Carlsen went downstairs and introduced himself to the man sitting in the waiting room.

'Now, I understand that you have some information on the Olive Adams case?'

'Well, yeah but not so much information as something more solid which you might be interested in, like,' the man replied, rummaging around in a grubby carpet bag which lay on the table.

He then produced a knife which he placed in front of Carlsen. It was mostly covered in dirt, particularly on the wooden handle, but the DI could see traces of a dark substance staining a slightly curved blade.

'Where did you get this, Mr Collins?'

'Well, I'm the gardener to old Mrs Richards at the next-door house to the Adams woman, and I came around to her side to finish trimming the yew hedge, with her sister's permission, you understand. Well, it were very thick and I was cutting it right back, like, and I spotted this thing right at the bottom covered in leaves and dirt. I thought perhaps you might be interested, being as seeing you've never caught no one and never found the knife what did her in neither.'

'Yes, we certainly are,' responded the DI. 'If possible, we'd like a statement from you and fingerprints as well, just for elimination purposes, you understand. Also, it would be useful to borrow your bag as the knife's been in it, we'll give it back as soon as we've finished with it.'

'All right,' replied the man, 'provided these things don't take too long, like.'

After he had gone, Carlsen hurried back to the DCI's office and spoke to Martin, carefully placing the knife on the DCI's blotting pad.

'I wondered what you were doing. John. I want you to take this personally to Worcester and get the brains to work on it, I'll let them know you're coming. This could just be the break we've been waiting for; this job's been going on long enough.'

The following afternoon, there was the anticipated phone call to DCI Martin.

'Maggs at Worcester here, sir, regarding that knife sent over with Mr Carlsen. It seems that it's the weapon involved in the murder. The curve on the blade fits the shape of the cuts suffered by Adams and there is also a slight distortion towards the end, which is also represented by marks at the edge of the various wounds. We have not been able to lift any prints from the knife or get anywhere with the substance on the blade which is dried blood. Too much time has passed, and in any case the blood is heavily contaminated by dirt which must have been picked up when it was dumped. But one other interesting thing, we've cleaned the handle and found a two-figure number scratched in the wood on both sides but I've no idea what it represents. If someone wants to come over today, I'll give 'em the knife back plus my official report.'

'Well, that's what I call progress, now all we've got to do is sort out the significance of that number and maybe we've got our suspect,' commented the DCI rubbing his hands together.

'Anyway, John, arrange for the goods to be collected, will you?'

Later in the day, the knife having been returned to Malvern, Martin and Carlsen examined it in the latter's office.

'So, what do you think about the number on the handle, sir, what could it be?' Carlsen remarked, turning the weapon over in his hand.

Martin puffed out his cheeks and shrugged.

'I don't know, who writes numbers on knives? Scouts, somebody in the army? I've really no idea at the moment but we've got to work it out somehow.'

'Well, it looks as if Worcester are coming to our rescue, sir, in a manner of speaking. I notice in orders that a couple of extra DCs are being posted here next month. By the look of their warrant numbers, they've got a few years' experience between them. Pity they didn't send 'em before, otherwise we wouldn't have needed quite so much outside help.'

Martin suddenly stood up, almost tipping his chair over.

'What did you just say, John?'

Carlsen looked puzzled.

'I mentioned that the extra DCs they're sending us look as if they could be useful with their length of service.'

'Yes,' replied Martin quietly, staring into space, 'it's not so much warrant numbers; you don't suppose, you don't suppose,' he repeated?'

Chapter 25

That evening, Detective Constable Edward Empson was sitting over a beer in The Unicorn.

'Hello, Eddie,' said a voice, 'haven't seen you for a while.'

Empson looked up, it was a former colleague from pre-Malvern days, James Clark.

'Hello, Jim, what are you doing here? Sit down and have a pint, what are you having?'

'Oh, a bitter will do, thanks. I've just been visiting my old mum who lives around the corner. She's not so well these days, what with her arthritis and all that but there we are.'

'Oh, really? I could pop around and see her sometime if you like, Jim,' volunteered Empson, 'where does she live?'

'Along the Worcester Road, may be you could some time,' replied Clark, somewhat surprised, 'so you're still at Malvern nick, I suppose?' he asked as the landlord busied himself at the pump.

'Yeah, still there.'

'It's been a bit busy, hasn't it, what with your guvnors not being unable to solve that old girl's murder?'

'Yeah, that's really got 'em foxed that one,' Empson replied with a slight smile.

'But that's their problem,' he went on, 'anyway, I think old Fowler retires soon so why should he worry? He's never been quite the same since he was done over by that Clover bloke. So, what are you doing these days?'

'Oh, still plodding around at Worcester CID, but if you hear of any more vacancies over here, let us know, I could do with a move. Used to be sleepy valley, Malvern, but not anymore, it'd make a nice change. According to orders, a couple more of our blokes who've been at Worcester for a while are coming over here anyway, so I won't be getting a transfer this time around.'

The two continued to reminisce for a while and then Clark left.

Empson stayed put and became increasingly maudlin but had a sudden change of mood and began to smirk to such a degree that the landlord became aware of this sudden change and glanced at the man curiously.

'Something has obviously tickled you pink,' said the landlord after a while, 'you didn't look too happy a while ago.'

'Well, it's amazing how certain things can cheer you up when they pop into your head,' replied the detective, 'pull us another pint, Reg.'

'And what things might they be, Mr Empson?' the man asked.

'Ah, well, that's a secret,' the detective replied, tapping the side of his nose.

He was still smiling some half an hour later when, clamping his hat firmly on his head, walked out into the evening air to return to his lodgings but felt unaccountably uneasy when he heard the sound of a car moving slowly behind him in the gloom. He turned around as the Malvern CID car with sidelights on overtook him on the opposite side of the road and glided slowly away. He waved but received no response.

'Funny, what are they up to?' Empson muttered to himself, having briefly noted that the car contained two men. He then heard the sound of the car turning around and then returning, this time on his side of the road. It moved abreast of him and drew slowly to a halt a little way ahead. In a few moments, a man emerged from the front passenger seat and blocked the detective's way. It was Detective Superintendent Fowler. DCI Martin then got out from the driver's side and moved behind Empson.

'What's going on, sir, has something happened?'

Ignoring the question, Fowler spoke quietly, 'I think that the next time you stab an old lady with a knife, Empson, and then bash her over the head, you'd better make sure your old collar number isn't scratched on the knife handle.'

Empson's mouth opened slightly and he framed his lips, as if to say something but nothing came out. He started to sweat and removed his hat whilst continuing to look nervously at the two men. He was then grabbed by Martin and pushed into the back of the police car with Fowler sitting beside him.

'Edward Empson I'm arresting you on suspicion of the murder of Olive Adams on 27 October 1937.'

Fowler then recited the caution.

'Do you understand?' he asked.

The detective nodded and shivered a little but said nothing.

DC Empson was taken to Worcester police station and interviewed at length by Fowler and Martin but refused to acknowledge his involvement in the death of Olive Adams, claiming that although the knife was his, he had lost it some weeks before the murder.

He also denied any involvement in the death of Fred Green at Worcester.

About a week after Empson's arrest, DS Roberts was reluctantly returning to work from leave and tramped slowly up the stairs to Malvern CID office imagining that a cluttered desk would be awaiting him and a thousand and one other jobs that he probably should have done before he went on holiday. He arrived in the office, and noticing a distinct atmosphere, glanced at two detectives who were working there. His arrival was barely acknowledged.

'Sergeant Roberts, in my office please,' called DCI Martin, who was standing looking bleakly out of the window. A few seconds later, Carlsen joined them.

'I hope you've had a good holiday, sarge, because we've got some bad news for you. Since you've been away, DC Empson has been arrested and charged with the murder of Olive Adams, best you hear it from us first,' announced the DCI quietly.

Robert's mouth fell open and stayed open for several seconds.

'Sir? But why?'

'We found the knife that killed her or, more accurately, the gardener from next door found it hidden in the bottom of a thick hedge. That's why we missed it, plus no dabs or anything and the bloodstains on it could not be used for evidence they'd been there too long. The clincher was that there were two numbers cut into both sides of the wooden handle: number 45, which turned out to be Empson's collar number from when he was a uniform PC. Several people attest to the fact that he owned the knife years back, flashed it about quite a bit, was very proud of it from all accounts.

'He won't have the murder, alleges that he lost the knife some time before the attack and therefore says that somebody else was responsible for the killing. Says he'll take his chances with a jury. Also denies anything to do with the death of an old boy some years ago at Worcester who was involved in one of his cases but we think he'll go down for our murder. We think he might have been up to a little bit of thieving and was having a look at the Adams property when he was challenged and recognised by Olive Adams, having known Empson from way back when she was involved in a complaint against him. She must have threatened to report him and he then chased her up the stairs in the house, stabbing her as she went before finally killing her with the vase. He must have dropped the knife and accidentally kicked it under the hedge as he scarpered, didn't have time to look for it. There must have been a fair bit of blood on him so he was lucky not to be spotted on his way home but it was dark anyway. But we found some bloodstains of the same blood group as Olive Adams on his clothing, some of which he'd tried to burn and also in the lace holes of his shoes, so that clinched it. No sign of any gloves blood stained or otherwise though and he denied any knowledge. Said that he didn't know how her blood had got onto him, suggested it was a stitch up, which of course it wasn't. Either way, I reckon it'll finish him with any half-savvy jury.

'Anyway, we will never know the exact train of events because the woman's dead and he's not telling; so there we are, sorry, sarge.'

'Well, I never liked the man, sir, had a temper on him and I'd heard rumours, as you did, but I never would have believed that he was capable of that. He was a good detective but I hope the bastard swings.'

Edward Empson was tried for the murder of Olive Adams at Worcester Assizes to which he pleaded not guilty but was convicted and found to be insane. He was committed to a secure mental institution for an indefinite period.

'This is a sad day for the job and all of us at Malvern nick, John,' reflected DCI Martin, 'but I suppose it's a good thing he wasn't married and doesn't seem to have had much family.

'I still can't believe that one of our own could do what he did, and right under our noses as well. Almost as bad, we will never know if he did in that old man, Green, at Worcester but it's quite likely. No peace for his family. Since Empson was nicked, I've often wondered why he crossed swords with Olive Adams before she ever came to Malvern, it has to be that incident that triggered her murder. Like Leticia Glass, it seems that he never forgot a slight and maybe there was something about old people that he didn't like. Anyway, the jury concluded that he was insane at the time he killed poor old Olive so we have to accept that, but he was lucky to escape the hangman. Come on, let's go down the pub, I've had enough of this place.'

'Do you know, John,' Martin commented as they settled down near the pub fire, 'my pension is coming down the road soon and when it appears around the corner, I fancy I might just put my papers in? This whole business has got to me, firstly Glass, then Austen and now this bloody man, Empson. They were obviously funny in the head but at least the Glass woman and Austen were never guilty of murder; although I suppose the latter was in a manner of speaking. I know I go on about it too much and I do realise this business has affected you as well.'

'Yes, of course it has, but for your part you've surely got a few more years in you yet? In fact, I hope we both have,' Carlsen responded a little taken aback.

'Oh, I don't know, I still wonder why I allowed myself to be taken for a fool by that Austen woman with all my experience. It's knocked the stuffing out of me for a while now to say nothing of this latest business. Somehow, it's made me more cautious, which may be a good thing in this job but caution has never really been in my nature. You've got to take some chances, but I'm not sure I've got it in me anymore. Trouble is, there's another war coming and I can see the powers that be keeping on old bastards like me for the duration.

'And what about you, John?' Martin continued, 'if you put in for the next one, I could have a word in the right quarters and keep the chair warm for you; I can't think of anyone better qualified.'

'I'm not sure I want the next one, guvnor, thanks all the same, I've got a few years to go yet and I'm happy the way I am. But as you say, there's another war coming, so God knows what'll happen.'

'Well, you might change your mind.'

The two men talked some more before Martin got up from his chair.

'Nice and warm in here, John, but we'd better go back to the nick in case the chief constable thinks we've retired without telling him.'

'Oh, there you are, Mr Martin,' said Sergeant White as the two men walked through the door, 'a Lady Clemenson has had a load of jewellery nicked at the Abbey Hotel, could you take a look, sir? DS Roberts is out on a job and I can't find anyone in the office.'

'Oh, no, not that dotty old girl again. The last time she reported her jewellery missing, we found it in a shopping bag under her bed but just in case any known suspects running about, sarge?'

'No, sir.'

'All right, come on, John, let's have a nice little walk up the hill, shake off the effects of that brown ale you made me drink.'